A Sailing Legacy

Adventures of the Sea Captain

by Rada Lyubomirova

***

Neurodivergent Version

***

Alpha Eureka Edukasia, Inc., 2023.

First published on September 13th '2023

Digital Version ISBN: **978-1-963038-66-8**

Paperback Print ISBN: **979-8-9884575-7-2**

Hardcover Print ISBN: **978-1-963038-08-8**

Travel Version ISBN: **978-1-963038-01-9**

Neurodivergent Version ISBN: **978-1-963038-09-5**

***

Alpha Eureka Edukasia, Inc., DE, USA.

https://www.compendiapublishing.com

FAIR WARNING

This publication contains explicit language, explicit romantic scenes, and uncommon courtship. Readers' discretion is advised.

This work of fiction is NOT suitable for minors. The age limits may vary from one area of jurisdiction to another.

In the absence of clear guidance and/or limitations from the governing bodies, the publisher and the author suggest that 21 years of age be the minimum age for reading this publication.

DISCLAIMER

This book is a work of fiction that draws inspiration from a Southeast Asian folktale and history, with some parts added for a dramatic purpose.

The literary work might be a disruption to the later wave of feminism around the time of publication. By the end of this book, readers will understand the reason, but not before that. If it starts a discourse on redefining feminism, then this book serves its purpose.

This work of fiction is for entertainment purposes only and is NOT to be treated as a matter of fact or as the ground for theories. This publication may be treated as a subject to study in the language arts, literature, culture, psychology, or any other related department or faculty.

The manuscript and art cover of this literary work are not generated by artificial intelligence and may NOT be utilised for AI training without the written permission of the copyright owner.

Also by Rada Lyubomirova

To understand who the Great One and his wife are,
kindly read the **"LILITH AND SAMAEL"** book series.
Book 1—A Story of the Twin Flame
Book 2—The House of Alchemists
Book 3—The Guardian Prince of Rome

***

SLAVA DEITY
Lord of the Underworld: A Paranormal Shifter
Romance of Veles
Springtime Birth and Wintertime Rebirth:
A Psychic Paranormal Romance of Yarilo and Morana

MATERNAL HOUSES

An Anthology of Polyamorous Families
Lady of the Rebels: Polyandry in the Exile
A Sailing Legacy: Adventures of the Sea Captain
The Watchman of Salt and Dust:
Svyatoslav Bratva Romance

***

THE ARK OF THE SHADOW-WORKERS:

Legend, Myth, and Folklore Retelling
A Sailing Legacy: Adventures of the Sea Captain
Princess Mandy and Her Watchman: A Fake
Marriage Bodyguard Romance
The Watchman of Salt and Dust: Svyatoslav Bratva
Romance
Firebird: A Second Chance Romance of the
Pilot-in-Command
House of the Sailors: Pirates of the North

Dedication

To the good girl who has been called 'a bitch' for working in a male-dominated industry. No need to get grumpy about them; just remember how you've become your Master's whore in bed.

1

Common Ground

"Ah, I was right to come home for summer break. I almost didn't want to," said Tama when he found his father sitting on the sofa. He surely saw me sucking his father's cock. "Hey, Dad. Mind if I join?"

"Help yourself, son. She's been a brat the entire morning." Aroha pulled my hair back, making his thick cock pop out of my mouth. "He's been good with his study, so you need to give him some rewards."

"Yes, Daddy."

"Crawl to him, Mia." The forty six years old father slapped my cheek with his cock. So I turned my face towards the twenty years old son.

He walked closer to the common room. With me kneeling before him, he brushed my hair like a pet owner. The jeans restrained his hardening cock but didn't conceal it so well. "My dad's been punishing you, yeah? Sit like a good pet, Mia. Or I'll be punishing you much harder than my dad."

Like a good pet, I did as he said. He removed his backpack and put it beside him. Tama was into rock climbing. His orange ropes were tied to the front of his backpack. Those hazel eyes caught me staring at those ropes. "What? You want the ropes?"

My parted lips only showed him nothing but my desire. I licked my bottom lip before nodding to him.

"Take your clothes off. Keep the bra and knickers on." After I took my clothes off, Tama put his ropes around my neck. He made a knot in the front, just like a tie. "Stand up now."

He slipped the rope under the joint of my bra and made another knot before pulling both sides under my breasts and around towards my back. "Turn around. Show my dad how firm these knots are. He taught me about these when I was little. Surely, he never expected me to make them for our pleasures."

By pulling my hair up, I gave Tama a free way to tie me from behind. After pulling both ends under my bra, he made another loop above my breast. The friction forced me to let out a moan. He continued to make another knot in the front. His father watched us while stroking his cock.

"Do you like it, Daddy?"

"You look beautiful like that, restrained." His fist was firm, pushing out that shiny bead of precum that provoked my thirst. "Look what you've done to me."

A knot now sat on my lower abs. Tama slipped the ropes under my knickers. After both ends were pulled around to the back, another knot was made above my arse under the fabric. His last knot connected the loop that was wrapping around my waist.

"Spread your legs. I need my ropes soaked with your juice." Tama pulled both ends in between my legs to the front and spread them apart. Each end was tied to each side of my hips. "There you are, tied beautifully. You'll make a good pet for us, if only you're not in a hurry to catch your ship. Let my dad check your ropes, pet."

The friction burned my folds so good as I was crawling back towards Aroha. The wetness of my arousal soaked these ropes as his son wished. The common room was already filled with my moans.

"Daddy?" In between Aroha's legs, I knelt down. As he checked his son's knots, I felt some parts rubbing my folds again.

"*What a cunt!*" It betrayed me for showing them how much I wanted to be degraded. I was supposed to be the woman in command, not under someone's command.

He scooped the arousal from me and smeared it on my lips. "Turn around. Suck my son's cock with some juice on your lips." After I turned around towards his son, he pulled my knickers to the centre.

Tama's built up chest was already bare, showing all his muscles. He took off his belt and pulled his jeans half way to free his cock. Aroha squeezed and massaged my arse well while Tama fucked my throat. When his son pulled back from me, two spanks landed hard on my arse. Each cheek had its turn.

Tama pulled my hair back and said in my ear, "That's what dad does to a brat. He hits hard, so this pussy better be drenched before he punishes you harder." He was feeding me again with his half length when his father's finger filled me. Then another finger pushed inside to massage my walls. When the third finger stretched me, my whimper filled their common room.

Tama's entire length was shoved down my throat. His strokes became feral. His right hand kept my head in place by pulling my hair. The other hand held my throat to feel himself inside me. He ensured that his cock reached me deeply.

Another slap landed on my arse when I was gagging. "Breathe with your nose. We need to use that throat well," said Aroha. So his son followed his command, fucking my throat harder.

My ears listened to the wet sound of Aroha's three fingers stretching my tunnel. It made me grind back towards his hands. "Want some juice, son?"

"Sure." His son pulled his cock from my swollen lips. Those fingers were now out of me. Aroha scooped up my wetness. He pulled me back by the hair to sit and watch him give his fingers to Tama—fingers that were covered with my glistening juice. It was just like watching a father feed his hungry child with so much care.

"Thanks for the tasty juice, Dad. But let's see if she can squirt more juice." Both of them ripped open condoms to wear.

Aroha freed my breasts from the black lace bra. "Drown my cock with your wet pussy." He pulled my waist up. He sat me down so fast on his lap. That thick cock painfully ripped apart my core for good this time.

"Daddy, you're thick." My whimpering moan surely sent them into madness.

He squeezed my breasts from behind. "Tama can lick you better." So his son started lapping along my slit; his fingers moved up to pinch my nipples.

My tunnel was full for good. My clit was being eaten so well. My breasts become toys for four rough hands.

"Slap her breasts hard, son," said Aroha. That order made Tama growl while eating me. The vibrations tortured my already swollen clit. The son did what the father ordered. They made me their training equipment.

"Harder! You don't hold back! Like this." Aroha's hard slap landed on me. My tears fell down my cheeks. Then Tama's harder slaps landed on both of my breasts. The father sounded so proud of his son.

"Now, come for my son, Mia. You were being such a brat the entire day. More juice for my son."

A feral tongue attacked my clit as the father's thick cock stroked my pussy up to my hilt. My arms wrapped around Aroha's neck behind me, hanging onto him so I wouldn't slip. I felt so full and consumed by this father-son duo. And I released myself to them.

Tama slurped every drop of me while his father was still inside of me. When he kissed me after, he let me taste myself. "Clean me with your tongue. Taste how good you are."

After a slap stung it, Aroha pinched my too sensitive clit. He then lifted my thighs to spread my opening wider. He wanted his son to stretch me even more.

"Please, Daddy, I'm already full. Please." My begging didn't seem to bother him.

"When my dad wants something, he gets it. If he wants your pussy to be ruined, your pussy will be ruined apart."

"Please I—"

My neck was suddenly wearing a necktie; it was Tama's hand. Then another cock entered my tunnel halfway. I wanted to cry out. But I wanted both cocks more. "It's full. Please, I ca—Oh."

"Then tell us to stop if you really want us out. You either get both me and my son inside your little cunt, or you don't get any of us at all."

"Do you want us both in or both out? Use your words, Mia. Tell us what you want." Tama stared at my lips, waiting for some answers. His lips were so close to mine. I could still smell my release on him, making me crave my own remaining taste.

"No, don't leave me. But I'm full. Daddy's thick."

"Then you need to beg like a good girl."

"Please. I need both of you inside me." My cry for being stretched hurtfully became a begging cry.

"Is that what you want? You want us in?" Once he saw me nodding, his halfway cock thrust in with one fast stroke. He joined his father, who was already making me full.

Aroha pulled the ropes on my lower abs. My hips were burned by the pull. "It seems like our little Mia has learnt her lesson. Legs, wider."

While leaning back against his chest, I held the back of my knees high with my forearms. I was almost there again, so close to my second orgasm. Their strokes became harder and faster because of how my inner walls clenched them. They sent me to my second release.

"That's our good girl," Aroha said.

Two sets of hands slapped my face and breasts in turns. Their strokes continued until I could feel them softening inside me. One followed the other.

Tama lifted me from his father. He sat me on his lap while he sat himself to the right of his father. While resting my head on Tama's shoulder, I felt Aroha's fingers brushing my hair.

"You see, it wasn't that hard to be our good girl," he said to me. Aroha kissed my lips gently. "Do you want me to cook something for you? How about pasta before you catch your ship? Your favourite one?"

"Yes. Pasta would be nice," I said while cupping his jaw. Somehow, letting myself be spent in this warm house made me feel so grounded.

"I can shower you while Dad cooks. No worries, I'll drive you to the port, so you can rest in the car," Tama said.

2

The Ark of the Shadow-Workers

There was only one other ocean liner to set sail nowadays; she connected the UK and the US. The other one was her sister, who was only reborn as a hotel.

As for the ship I commanded, I kid you not, she was young—less than a decade old. My baby girl was a brand-new ocean liner that the Great One himself had forged and built. She was built to sustain the raging ocean, enough to build lives of our own in the ocean.

The rain was distilled into drinkable water. Desalination systems were installed as the secondary system if the rain wasn't happening. The clean water systems were thoughtfully built for the living on board, humans, plants, and animals. If you thought a greenhouse on a ship was a fantasy, try believing in an entire farm at the top of Slava. That was her name—a 400 metres long and 60 metres wide ship.

She could carry up to 5,000 passengers, but we kept it down to a maximum of 3,500. Although I'd prefer a maximum of 2,500 of our kind, the extra 1,000 guests were needed to fulfil commercial purposes. And expensive she was for the guest; only the filthy riches could afford her.

With the hybrid power ready to work, we kept our schedule sharp. As long as I could catch her while travelling from place to place, she saved me so much on concessions. I hopped on her even when I wasn't in a rotation. Each member of the ship crew was scheduled for a thirteen-week duty rotation on the thirteen-level ship. There were still a couple more weeks until my duty started. I caught her schedule in Auckland instead of starting rotation right away in Australia. There I saw her, getting ready to sail.

Mostly, I travelled with my first and third mates, but not always. When we didn't, we found comfort somewhere else on our own journey. The father and son earlier were one of those comforts. Most of the time, we ended up together again. We shared our bridge as much as we shared our bed.

"Ugh, you smell like sex! Did they fuck you raw?"

"No. Only you two do that," I said to Sandec.

"Glad you caught both of us here. Otherwise, you'd go straight to being a demanding captain again." He grabbed my waist closer. "We need to remind you who is in command of this body."

"Our cunt better be drenched by the time the horn goes off." Joe-Kung grabbed my arse as if no one was watching.

There was something in their words that commanded my core to leak out my arousal. I breathed out a moan, and I didn't think my sunglasses were helping to conceal my desire.

My second-in-command was the younger brother, while my fourth in command was the older one. The brothers were three years apart, with me in between them. That was precisely where I belonged, sandwiched in between the two of them, with both their cocks fucking me raw.

"But I need to eat first, Joe."

"Then eat. Meats are ready to stuff our mouth here. I kind of miss how good it feels when you're gagged," he said while pressing his hardening cock against my side.

"Ooh, my cock's going to feel our cunt clenching when that gag happens," said Sandec. I could feel his cock against my other side—hardened as well.

These brothers suffocated me with my own desire. It wasn't like I disgraced the father-son, but the Ceolmund brothers had always been my family to share the bed with. We were siblings as seamen, a family by choice. We served each other with our bodies as soulmates, as we served the same duty and purpose as the shipmates.

When on board, the three of us were assigned to three operator suites away from each other. It was standard procedure to separate us. It was a 30-metre square suite that had one bedroom, a bathroom, a small common room, a kitchen, and a dining area. This class was where most of the shadow-workers lived. The operator suites laid across Deck 9, on the forward and aft of Decks 8, 7, and 6.

Slava was designed to support the shadow-workers in their projects. A floating sanctuary, hotel, and office at the same time. In today's terms, it was a floating home office. Operations were managed from the office in the middle of Decks 8, 7, and 6. It almost seemed like the operator suites were guarding those offices.

The leading shadow-workers lived in the leader suites on Deck 10. We called them the Watchmen. They lived in 50-metre square suites with two bedrooms, a bathroom, a common room, a dining room, and a kitchen.

The other class was the crew quarters, where the supporting crew lived. They didn't get to live in bunk beds like other ships placed their crew. Instead, they lived in personal 12-metre square rooms. Each member of the crew had a bed for two, a bathroom, and a table with two chairs. The quarters were laid along Deck 5, on the forward and aft parts of Deck 4 to Deck 0. The crews shared the common room and dining room at the restaurant. They were always welcomed at the cinema.

It was the Great One's wife who demanded it that way. While the Great One had our backs on duties and projects, his wife took care of us, the shadow-workers and the crew members. She cooked whenever she came to visit us.

"Three full meals and two light meals a day," Milady said.

3

Anchored Home

The horn was blowing when the Ceolmund brothers banged on my suite door. Opening the door, I immediately wore Sandec's hand as a necktie. He pushed me backwards to my dining table.

"You said that you needed to eat. Then eat Joe's cock like a good whore." He laid me on the table so that my neck was hanging on the opposite edge of the table.

Joe moved his hands along my exposed neck. He slapped me across the face with his other hand. "This throat needs to be filled with good meat." He pulled my shirt and bra to my neck roughly. While he was playing with my breasts, his brother was pinching my nipples.

"Ooo, Sandy, look at these handprints. Our little whore was used well. Wait, what are these? Ropes burns?"

Sandy smirked at my nod. "No, she hasn't. She's about to be used well... Right, Mia?" Sandy started to nibble my left nipple, and Joe followed on my right.

Both brothers were slapping my breasts to their liking. They licked me better after, only for my breasts to receive another regime of slaps again. Joe pulled my shirt and bra off me entirely, and Sandy pulled my jeans roughly without opening the button or zipper. Everything was down—my jeans, my knickers, and my shoes.

"Let me check our cunt. Did they fuck you well earlier?"

"They did, but not the way you two fuck me, Sandy."

"And why is that? Tell me why we need to fuck you raw." He spread my legs wide and bent my knees. His eyes were in awe at my glistening releases from the father-son fuck. "Look at our cunt, Joe. She must be coming more than once."

Joe slapped my clit hard that it stung. "Tell me, did they stuff their cocks together in our cunt? She looks swollen and stretched."

"Yes, they did. But I need you both. Please, Joe. I feel empty. Fill me up."

The brothers looked at each other before stripping themselves naked. "Second thought, no eating meat tonight." Joe lifted my arms, while Sandy lifted my legs. They carried me just like cargo handlers carry sacks. They swung and threw me onto the bed. They treated me precisely like an unworthy sack. In their hands, I was as cheap as a sack of flour to be shared to feed others.

Joe rolled me to lay on my stomach. My wrists were tied together on my back. "Ugh, more handprints, we can see." He massaged my arse with his caring hand before adding more handprints to it.

They slapped my arse in turns before bending my knees. From the corner of my eyes, I could see Sandy grabbing their belts. He stacked pillows underneath me, so my arse was raised high.

Joe kept caressing my skin so slowly. The friction from his hand started from my tied wrists up to my arms and back. It was just like the fire starter that ignited my whimper. "How many does our whore deserve? She let other cocks fuck our cunt. All without asking for our permission."

"That should be more than three each, Joe." Sandy ran his fingers through my hair before pulling it. "You think six is enough for making yourself a whore for other men?"

I shook my head. "I can take it."

"Ah, you must have given them so much pleasure. We'll remind you who this whore belongs to. If we want to share you, then we will share you. Eight each round, then."

My eyes were wide open in shock. "Each round? I thought it was eight from each of you. Please—" Before I finished begging, Sandy's belt landed on my arse. "One." Joe's belt took its turn after I started the counting. "Two." The brothers took their turn, one cheek at a time. "Three." I lifted my arse higher for my men. "Four." My tears started to drop. "Five." My pussy was leaking so much more juice for them. "Six." My whimper was echoing through the room. "Seven." I pushed my face against the pillows to silence my moans. "Eight."

Two tongues and mouths were lapping and eating my pussy. I spread my legs wide to give them more access. "Please, I need both of you inside me. They've stretched me already. Fill my empty hole, please."

"Wrong. It's not your hole. It's ours."

My hole was indeed filled with two generous fingers. Then another set of two fingers joined. Those fingers were stroking and fucking me in and out, making my pussy tighten. They massaged my walls in two different directions. When they felt me close, their massaging became rougher. Their tongues joined and made me so close to exploding. They became so wild, like starving animals. They sucked and drank my squirting release. Not a single drop was wasted.

While recovering, I was pulled to the edge. My arse dangled on the edge, only to receive another round of their belts. I started the count, "One." My punishment continued when another round started.

"Eight," I said when they completed the second round. "Please, Sandy, I need you both. Joe, please don't leave me empty." So they pulled me up to the middle of the bed again. This time, Joe rolled me on my back, and my tied up wrists were hurting under me.

After his thickness thrust inside me in one stroke, he rolled me to my left side. He gave Sandy a way in by pulling my thigh to his waist and squeezing my arse. "You want Sandy in our cunt or in our arse, Mia? Tell him which one to fuck."

"Pussy, Sandy. I want both of you to fill me with your cum. They used condoms earlier." As seafarers, we underwent regulated medical examinations. But Milady wanted us to have monthly sexual health tests. She figured out how wild we could be, fucking each other within or outside the institution.

Joe, Sandy, and I made an agreement when we first started sharing ourselves that we would only fuck wearing nothing with the three of us. We decided together to have an IUD inside me. I'd prefer pills, but they said that I easily get irritated on the job with hormonal birth control. Sometimes, I felt that they knew me better than I did.

Sandy stroked his length into my already-filled pussy, pushing me to slip out another moan from my mouth. "That's our whore, taking both of us." He squeezed my breasts one by one after setting my wrists free. Then he slapped them.

I wrapped my hand around the back of his neck. His hair in between my fingers felt smooth. "Come for us like a good whore. Drench our cocks in your squirts."

"You heard him, Mia. Be our good whore. What did they call you, then?" Joe slapped my cheek and wrapped my throat with his hand. "Did they call you their good girl? Hmm? Tell us."

"Yes, they called me their good girl." My moaning murmured into his mouth when Joe pressed his lips against mine. He and his brother fucked my pussy with a harmonious fucking rhythm. "But you two made me your whore. Then I should be used properly, like a whore."

"Open your mouth. Let your tongue out." Joe spat straight into my mouth and turned my face towards Sandy. "Spit into her, brother."

"Thank you," I said after swallowing their spit. My moan became louder as they kept thrusting my pussy just like I deserved it. Like a filthy whore, I begged them to get me off the second time. "Harder, please."

They steered me through the wave of pleasure. "What a good whore! Now give us another one." Sandy's hands slipped in between Joe and me. His fingers rubbed my overly sensitive clit.

"I can't anymore. Ummh—"

"Yes, you will. We want more," Joe said. He lifted my right leg high for them to fuck me deeper. "A good whore gives us what we order."

They didn't even give me a moment to recover from the second one. Now their cocks were fucking me so wildly in the same hole. Sandy's fingers were feral when rubbing me. They pushed me to cry while coming so hard.

One by one, the Ceolmund brothers pumped their cum into me. I felt nothing but warmth. Even if the three of us might look like a sandwich, they make me feel at home. They rolled me over to lay on my back. When their cum leaked out of me, they scooped up the mixture of our pleasure to feed me with it.

"Taste how good we are together," Sandy said.

"Only our good whore gets our cum. Remember, this cunt belongs to me and Sandy."

We spent some time being wasted on our releases. My pussy was sore from being used so well today. They showered me and washed my hair after we recovered from our orgasms. After that, Joe made supper for us while Sandy took care of me after a full day of being fucked.

They fed me in bed and showered me with kisses after each bite. When I felt full, I snuggled deeply under them. I was fast asleep in their arms.

For the next two days, we mostly spent our time in our rooms. They gave me some time to rest, but at night, one of the brothers took turns coming to my room and cuddling me to sleep. I woke up every morning with my clit being eaten as breakfast. Both of them demanded to drink my release to start their day, but they gave my pussy some time to heal. They knew my body so well, I couldn't ask for more from them. On duty, I was their captain, but in the bedroom, I was their whore. I'd prefer to be anchored this way.

4

The Fourth Day

I woke up on the fourth day to Sandy's messy, spiky hair. His hair was soft, and I liked brushing his hair with my fingers. His body wasn't soft. He's 185 centimetres tall and a gym bro who was also into martial arts.

When my father took Sandy under his wing, he sent him to a defence class, saying that I needed a bodyguard. And that was what Sandy had been doing ever since. He had been protecting and defending me. When anyone ever had a crazy thought about attacking me, Sandy always had my back.

In some areas, Slava had narrow aisles that could only fit one person. When Sandy walked behind me, he usually tapped my head for being so small compared to him. By 'usually,' meaning when there was no one around us. He demanded that everyone respect the captain. Though I knew that it was his way of telling everyone that no one was allowed to disrespect me, I knew that he and Joe were the only people who could disrespect and degrade me.

"You okay, baby girl? You woke up so early." He woke up to my hand cupping his face and to my kiss on his lips. He slipped his forearm between my thighs, towards my back. With it, he pulled me closer to him. His morning wood pressed against my core. "Baby, are you all right? Did you have a nightmare? Hmm? It's all right, baby, I'm here."

I poured kisses on his concerned face. "No, I didn't have a nightmare. I'm all right. I'm just staring at you like a weird dude. Did I scare you?"

"You scared the shit out of me when I couldn't find you in the crowd. It might be a good idea to wear bright clothes and a hat. You know, like the late Queen of England. She was old, but that didn't hold her back from wearing something bright."

"*She.was.old?* And this is the way you remind me that I'm old?"

"Yeah, yeah, I've got a thing for older women. Allow it. What I'm saying is that it's gonna be easier for me to find you if you're missing in the crowd."

"Aww, you missed me. Did your cock miss me, too? I kind of missed him."

"Of course he missed you, baby. These past days were torture, but we wanted our pussy to heal first.

So that we can ruin it again." He savoured my lips softly.

His hand found its way under my tank top and rubbed my breasts. "Are they hurt, baby girl?" His lips curled into a smile when I shook my head. His kisses traced down from my lips to my neck and chest, and finally to my already hardened nipples.

Sandy could be rough with me. He loved to hurt me in bed, but he gave me much more painful torture by being gentle like this. He wanted me to beg for his roughness.

My breasts took turns between his rubbing hands and lapping tongue. "Sandy, please. I missed you inside me. None of my holes were filled in the past few days."

He moved up to kiss me gently once again, torturing me even more. His large hand held the sides of my face. "I know, baby girl, but I like you begging. So I'll take my time with our holes."

His other hand slipped inside my knickers, only to find my wet folds. "So much juice only from my kisses? Oh, my pussy really missed me." He didn't give my tunnel any fingers, only playing my fold and clit slowly and gently.

"I want you to feel it when I come. Please, Sandy, oh... I'm already close."

He gave me his fingers to suck. "Taste how good you are, baby girl." He continued rubbing my clit and sucking my breasts. He sent me so close to my release and pushed my whimpers to roar in the room. So damn close, but then he pulled his fingers and licked them. Without saying anything, he left me and went to the bathroom.

Once he was out of the bathroom, he stroked his cock with his fist. "You want this cock filling our cunt? Hmm?" He continued stroking fast in front of me.

With my whining voice, I begged him to take me. "Your cock deserves to fuck me senseless. Fill me up to the brim, please." I watched him continue his strokes, harder and faster.

"Get naked and be a good whore." His stroking continued while watching me take off my clothes. "Spread open your fold with your fingers. I need to see how needy our cunt is."

My pussy leaked out more wetness by watching him catch his release. "Please, Sandy."

"What a worthless piece of meat with holes to fuck. Nothing but holes to be filled with our cum. Remember that." All his length thrust in one stroke. He fucked me fast and hard without building me up. He just used me to catch his release, just like a whore. Then I could feel his warmth inside me. With a few pumps, he filled my empty hole.

He whispered in my ear, "We've made some plans for you, baby girl. Don't you dare touch yourself. Do you hear me, Mia? Do.not.give yourself a release!" He winked at my nod before making me clean his cock with my tongue.

Once he was fully clothed, he left me on edge and alone in my room. He just made me desperate for a release.

5

Silk

The three of us ate breakfast together in the restaurant. I decided to have bacon and eggs for breakfast before going to the gym. I wasn't entirely needing to burn my calories, but simply burning my craving for a release.

Sandy's gym time was much earlier than ours. Joe usually went pretty much at the same time I did my exercise. Joe had more lean, toned muscles than Sandy, who was built up like a tank.

While Sandy was a blank canvas, Joe was fully covered in tattoos. His art was well-covered in his smarter clothing. Being three centimetres shorter than his brother, people sometimes confused him for being the younger one. His hair was firm enough to be styled the smart way. Again, people might confuse him for being a gentleman. He didn't treat me like a good boy treats his girl in bed. He was *bad* at treating me like a princess in bed. He was *that good* at treating me like his whore.

I thought that Joe and I would train together at the gym, but we did not. I saw Joe at a glance through the mirror in the gym, continuing his session. After finishing my cardio, the active duty captain approached me. He just finished training and needed to have a word with me. We discussed how bad it was in Australia's base. The captain and I continued our conversation in the corner, away from anyone else.

When hearing the updates, I couldn't help but gasp and cover my mouth. He said that he would give a briefing to the shadow-workers in a few days but wanted to give me a heads up.

"You need to be ready for about 200 loadings from Melbourne and about 300 loadings from Freemantle. Most of them will need assistance."

"I'll find out how many of my crew are already on board. I think we need a joint table. How many will be unloaded?"

"About 250 for Melbourne and 400 for Freemantle. Oh, I almost forgot, the Great One and his wife will board after Freemantle on your duty rotation."

"We shall keep an eye on logistics between Melbourne and Freemantle. So I can adjust if we'd need any extra for my rotation."

"Yes, please keep me updated on how many logistics you'll need." He wiped off his face from the sweat.

"Did you hear anything about the Great One? How did he react to the incidents?"

"What...?! Why would you care about the Great One? You should be concerned about his wife. She's more like you, Captain. You two are unreadable and up for the long game. She scares the shit out of us, men. Beautiful for sure, but intimidating and giving us hell sometimes."

"Pfft... I didn't expect that anyone would scare this guy. Haha."

"Okay, Captain, I'm off."

As the active captain left, I walked towards Joe at his bench. He saw me coming. I was about to tell him about my briefing plan when he suddenly sat up. He then walked towards the other room with my arm in his hand. We entered the aerial yoga room, which I wasn't quite sure if anyone had ever used. They kept the room clean, and the equipment was well-maintained.

He locked the door after us and pinned me against it. "What was that all about with the captain? Did you let him touch you?"

"It was about work, nothing more. I didn't—"

"It didn't seem like it from what I saw. What was it with the laughter?"

"Joe, please. Just bantering between colleagues. I didn't mess around with him. I wasn't on guard because I knew that you were here to keep me safe."

"Do I need to remind you who you belong to? Tell me."

"You. I belong to you and Sandy." My shirt was suddenly pulled up to my waist.

With the yoga silk, he wrapped my waist. Using another set of silk, he wrapped and tied my wrists firmly. His wrapping made me stumble, hanging flat from my wrists to my waist. "And what are you to us, Mia? Hmm? Say it."

"Whore. I'm your whore." My shirt and sports bra were pulled open at the same time; he used them to wrap around my arms. My breasts were bare, facing the floor.

With his caring hands, he squeezed my breasts. The gentle touch of his fingers tortured my nipples by pinching them softly. At this moment, I realised what Sandy said earlier—that they'd planned something for me. "And what's our whore for?"

My upper body felt his touch everywhere. The friction from his slow movement electrified me to beg for his roughness. "To be used, Joe. Please."

He pulled me by the hair, exposing my neck. "You want to be used like a good whore?"

"Yes, Joe. Sandy used me earlier, but he didn't let me come."

"Did my brother fill our pussy with his cum earlier?"

"He did. I'm still pooled with it." My shorts were pulled down, along with my knickers.

"I better taste my brother inside you. Otherwise, I'm gonna torture this one, keeping our cunt empty for a very long time." He licked along my slit so gently that he made me more desperate. He ate mine and tried to suck Sandy's cum from my hole. "Mmh... Sandy tastes good inside you, Mia."

I let my head drop to see him. My upside down view was so clear; he was stroking himself. I spread open my legs, giving him a way to enter me. "Joe, my pussy is still empty."

"Wrong, it's our cunt. We will give you what we want to give you." It was his tongue, not his cock.

"I need your cock, Joe. Please, I'm close already. Let me get off, just once. Please."

He pumped his cock faster in his fist before entering my pussy hard. He didn't take time to stretch me with his thickness. His cock thrust into me, only to use me to catch his release. Sandy used me in the same way. "That's our good whore being used," he said after spraying his cum in me.

With his hand, he scooped up the cum that leaked out of me. Like a pet, I was fed. Once I licked and swallowed everything he gave me, my wrists were freed from the silk. He put his pants on but left me hanging by the waist. "Don't you dare touch yourself. You're not allowed to come yet. Understood?"

"Understood." I was freed of the silk and left alone for the second time today. I was hanging on the edge, being used as their worthless whore.

6

The Briefing

My second mate happened to be on board as well.
He became a reserve for the active crew in this duty
rotation that none of us were aware of. Because
he would be an active crew member for the next
rotation, I asked him to join the briefing with the
three of us. Joe suggested that we should have our
briefing in his room instead of mine.

Lance-Ang Zhou's origins were unknown. An Asian
merchant sailor had raised him since he was found.
A few years ago, he took his DNA test to find out if
any of his family ties were ever in the system. His
result showed that he was indeed not Asian, as we
suspected from his appearance.

He had blond hair with green eyes and was 187
centimetres tall. He stood in the crowd amongst Joe
and Sandy with their brown hair. They called my
hair dirty blonde; probably it fit me considering how
I shared my bed with my mates. I was born with
amber eyes, while the Ceolmund brothers shared
similar brown eyes.

Lance was the typical sailor we saw in films, with ear piercings and tattoos showing on his arms. He kept his beard light, not as fully grown as Sandy or as clean-shaven as Joe. Sometimes I wondered if Lance ever knew about my companionship with Joe and Sandy.

I briefed my crew on what the active captain told me at the gym this morning. "Even if the captain said that there would be 500 loadings heavier, it would take days to reach Melbourne, let alone Freemantle. Joe, can we request medical logistics for 600 when porting in Freemantle? For precautions."

"That one, I need to confirm how much they already have right now. But I'll keep up with their inventory between Melbourne and Freemantle," said Joe.

Lance made a pensive pause. "Can you confirm to the captain if they're going to port in Adelaide?"

"Ah, yes, that makes sense. Work with Sandy and try to keep track of the loadings as well, and how bad they are."

Sandy responded, "I can try to contact the rest of our deck crew to give them a heads up. But since we don't know how bad it is yet, I won't be too specific."

I nodded in agreement with Sandy. "Lance, if we make several extra stops after Freemantle, well, I'm talking about *if* the situation escalates in the west region. If we port in Geraldton, Hedland, and Dampier, can we still catch our schedule for Lombok?"

"I need to calculate the alternatives. Assuming they're going to port in Adelaide, we'll be expecting a delay even for Freemantle. Let me build scenarios while you're confirming their routes."

"Yes, I'll confirm it first, early in the morning. You can't waste any time making unnecessary plans." I sighed before getting away with the fairy. For a moment, I went back to my last conversation with an old friend.

Joe broke our silence. "Mia, where did you go? If there's something alerting you, then you need to let us know ahead of time. I also need to measure the risks. So Lance can have more reliable alternatives."

"Oh, no. Nothing about our duties. Do you remember my friend Mandy?"

"Ah, yeah. The one from London. Didn't she return to Lombok with her father?"

"She did. It's been almost a year now, I think. Well, I phoned her in Auckland. I told her that we'd be staying in Lombok for a night. She's..." I paused for another sigh. "Rather concerning. I don't know what it is, but she didn't sound like herself. A bit... off."

Lance replied, "I'll make some alternative routes. Hopefully, we can port not so late, even if we're behind schedule. So you two can catch up on some stories. Not only for her, but for you, too."

"I appreciate that, Lance. Her father sort of put her in a tower. He hired a bodyguard, an ex-military. To follow her around if she wasn't in the 'tower.' Although she said about him being cute, she's a free spirit, you see."

Sandy raised his eyebrows. "Considering we have many ex-military shadow-workers, I don't remember any of them being cute. Well, hopefully, she's okay. She sees you as her sister. You give her a big hug whenever you two meet. It must be hard for her after her mum passed away."

"That's my concern. Her father, well, this is how she told me... He set her up for a marriage. She's an only child, and he didn't remarry. Can you imagine an only daughter managing his company?"

"That one, I can understand. He's concerned about who's gonna take care of her when he's gone. But I'm not sure arranging her marriage would be best for her."

"That's my point, Joe."

Quickly, he changed the subject, so I wouldn't be too concerned about Mandy. "Anyway, about logistics. If we make extra portings and they make another port, I don't think 600 medical logistics is enough. But we'll confirm their current inventory in the morning. Can you give a heads up to the captain so I can move easier? The inventory crews sometimes don't make it easy to look around."

"Of course, I'll give him a heads up."

Sandy followed, "Let's go fish them up. I'll contact our deck crew, and I'll try to confirm if any other department's crew is on board. We'll need every resource we can get."

"Does anyone have any idea what the fuck is happening in the headquarters? Is it in one base or bases across Australia?"

"Lance, you know it isn't our place to ask for too many specific details. Sometimes it isn't what it seems. The Great One and his wife have so many hidden layers that we don't quite see them with our bare eyes."

"Owh, now you're talking about hidden layers. I used to think there was only black and white. Then I found out that some of the projects came from whatever government. They work in the shadows while those governments keep their hands clean. Yeah, those governments can clean my arse. And guess who's the one fishing out loadings from the sea? Us. Shadow-workers, huh? Seems that they're treated as disposables."

"Whoa... hold your horses, bruv. Don't you have a date with Amma? You can't seem upset when you see her. Otherwise, she'll be feeding you more." Sandy loved to tease Lance at any chance he got. They were quite close during their training.

"My goodness, Mia, can you help get me off the hook? Bless Amma. She's got a kind heart, that lady. Don't get me wrong, but she's been hooking me up with her niece, Emilia. The fuck am I gonna do with a 22-year-old freshgrad probie?"

"Lance, I thought you loved Amma's cooking. What did you say? Homemade auntie's dish? You know, if you're with Emilia, you can always get to eat Amma's cooking more on the ground."

"Really, Mia? You, too? Unbelievable."

"Speaking of food, I'm cooking for tea. This ungrateful baby brother surely won't be cooking. Mia, are you joining us?"

"Yes, sure, Joe."

Lance stood up to leave the suite. "Okay, see you tomorrow then," he said before closing the door behind him.

7

On Edge

"Let Joe cook our meal. I'll prepare our dessert here." Sandy started to devour my lips with his. "I can smell our cunt's juice pooling. I'm sure Lance was smelling it, too. I wonder if he was hardened only by smelling it."

"What if he was, Sandy?" Once my clothes were peeled off, I was left with only my bra and knickers.

"Oh, I'm sure he was. He always has a *thing* for you." He smirked before leaving the room to get a bowl of water, a syringe, a tube of lubricant, and a tampon. "What? You never realised that?"

I heard Joe chuckling in the kitchenette. "And you two have known this for how long?"

"Since we were set up together, though Sandy caught it first. And we know that he.fucks.hard. That's probably why he's not into someone like Emilia."

Sandy laid me down on the table and took off my knickers. He prepared my arse with lubricant, then used the syringe to fill me with water. "What we do isn't for someone too young or too naive, Mia. 22-year-old Emilia hasn't seen the world enough to handle someone like us. You've seen the world enough. Besides, you sort of grew up with us, so you've seen the worst version of us."

"Hey, Sandy, did you fill her with warm or cold?"

"Why the fuck am I giving her warm water?"

"Yeah! We want our whore to cramp a bit. Fill her up, Sandy. I want her belly swollen like a baby mama."

Sandy emptied the first bowl of water. While waiting for him to get another round, I kept the water inside me. He kept filling my arsehole with more water, even if my belly already looked like it was six months pregnant. When he felt that I had enough, he shoved a tampon into my hole to keep the water inside. "Joe, you want to go first?"

"Watch the fire!" Joe pulled down my bra cups and freed my nipples. He cupped my breasts gently, just like when he used me in the yoga room. He pulled me until the back of my neck hung by the edge. The hardened cock was freed in front of my upside down face. His thickness filled me into the back of my throat. Those gentle hands of his rubbed my exposed neck to feel his cock inside of me. "Turn it off and join us. I'm close, and our whore's starving."

Joe turned to the other side of the table. Sandy got his way to fuck my mouth. His length kept pumping me while he paid attention to my drenched pussy and swollen belly. "So much juice from our cunt. Ooh, and this belly, I can tell you're gonna be a MILF one day."

"Do you think Lance's gonna like fucking our whore, Joe?" Because of his length, Sandy thrust my throat deeper than his brother. His thumbs rubbed my nipples so gently, contrary to his wild, thrusting cock.

Joe's gentle and slow thumb kept torturing my clit gently. "Of course he will. Our whore gets three holes. One hole for one man to use. Though it can be fun with two cocks in our cunt and another one in the arse," said Joe.

"Ugh, that sounds full. Do you want us to share our whore, Mia? He can fuck you even harder than us. That's from what we heard about him." Sandy pulled his cock from my mouth, waiting for an answer.

"Yes. If you don't mind, I want to be Lance's whore, too."

After hearing my answer, Joe started to thrust me with his cock. "But tonight, we're using our whore only for us." He pumped his release inside of me.

While sitting down, he watched Sandy take his turn fucking my pussy.

The Ceolmund brothers' cum filled me to the brim. They were sitting side by side, recovering from their orgasms. They watched me scoop up their release. Every drop of them covered my hand. I brought it to my mouth; theirs were mine to consume.

"That's our good whore hanging on the edge, craving to get off. Taste how good the three of us mixed together. Imagine what the four of us would taste like if Lance joined."

"Joe and I will eat first. You can use the bathroom. We'll feed our whore later."

"Pet eats last. Right, Sandy?"

"Sure do. No worries; we'll keep it warm for you. Keep yourself naked when you finish cleaning."

I let go of the water inside me and decided to take a shower. They had been edging me the entire day. I became so desperate to get a release from any of them.

"Crawl to us," Sandy said when I got out of the bathroom. They turned their seats towards me, with the dining table in between them. He held my face with care; his knuckles caressed my cheek.

"Mmh... Joe, it's delicious," I said after the first spoonful of risotto Sandy gave me. He was the type of man who provided. His cooking became his way of providing for us. He used white wine tonight. Even if the alcohol evaporated, I could still taste it.

Sandy opened the bottle of wine that Joe used for our meal. "Do you trust us, Mia? We'll make you finish this before fucking your arse." He showed me a quarter-emptied bottle of wine while I sat on the floor.

I nodded to them both. "I do," I said without any hesitation.

They made me drink the wine in between my feedings. They pushed their chairs closer to me so I could give them a handjob. After they finished feeding me, they continued giving me more wine. Even when they knew that my head was lighter than before, they were ready to use me one more time.

Joe pulled me to sit on his lap with my back against his chest. "Stretch her arse for me, Sandy." He lifted the backs of my knees to spread me wide.

"Ugh, look at our drunk whore here." A few drops of lubricant landed on his thumb. He smeared it around my arse. "Drunk and ready to be used in the arse." Sandy fucked my pussy in a few strokes before getting himself inside my arse.

"You still get the cramp?"

Nodding to Joe, I begged for a release. "Please, let me come."

"No way our whore is getting any release today. Maybe tomorrow. But let's see if she's being a good whore tonight."

Joe pinched my clit and said, "Maybe tomorrow we can let our whore come. Or maybe tomorrow we'll let Lance use our whore first."

Sandy kept thrusting my arse hard while rubbing my clit. His thrusts became faster until he sprayed his cum into me. He kissed my lips smoothly and lifted me to the sofa. While sitting underneath me, he opened my arse for his brother.

"Just once, please. I need to get off." My whimpering moan filled the room.

Joe started his turn to fuck my arse. His brother's cum was an extra lubricant for him. "What do you think, Sandy? Should we give our whore come tonight?"

"Nah... Don't think so. She's drunk. She won't feel her orgasm if she's wasted. You see, Mia, I want you to feel your damn-O. But we want you to be desperate first."

"Please, Sandy, Joe. You can't leave me on edge again. It's been too long."

Joe's thrusts became rougher. His thick cock stretched my arse at a fast pace. "Yes, we can, Mia. This whore is ours." Here, I felt him pumping his release.

I had lost count of how many times I had been edged. My head was so light from being drunk on alcohol and from being used so well. I was carried to bed. I felt them slurping the desperation from my pussy before I fell asleep.

8

Outburst

I woke up in the morning to my pussy being eaten by the Ceolmund brothers. Smooth eating as they continued to torture me with their gentleness.

They fed me their cocks for breakfast until they gave me my morning milk—their cum. They kept me on edge and denied me all over again.

Keeping myself busy helped with my orgasm deprivation for the day. I tried to get as much data as possible for our briefing. From the primary bridge, I went to the logistics and continued to the medical centre, confirming information and inventories. By dragging my feet back and forth across Slava, I managed to seal the leakage in my tunnel.

The four of us had our briefing in my suite in the late afternoon. Even after being used yesterday and running around the ship all day, I didn't realise how serious they were about sharing me with Lance. They sensed me trying to burn down my frustration. So my men said that I needed to slow down. They wanted me to focus on craving orgasm.

The active crew decided to port in Adelaide. With so much data to gather but so little information available, we ordered our meals for tea. We became heavily occupied with so much information and tried to plan and make alternatives ahead of our rotation. It was already late when we finished our briefing.

"You know I've been concerned about the three of you. Should I be concerned?" Lance took turns looking at each of us.

I acted as if I were unaware of what he was talking about. "Why should you be concerned about us?"

"You three are inseparable. The rest of us mostly keep our professional lives separate from our personal ones." He drank the beer from the bottle in his hand.

"Should they be separated? It can't be that bad. Sometimes it's about changing glasses to see better through different lenses," said Joe.

"So, *there is* something going on between you three?"

None of us said anything about our non-traditional companionship. Clinking the bottles of our beer should be enough to explain it all.

"Ugh... I didn't expect my suspicions to be true. Hey, I don't judge. I got my own bedtime story, so don't go after me." He shrugged his shoulders. "How can you two not be jealous, *if* you don't mind sharing?"

"Because we're good at sharing," Sandy said.

"Are you... good at sharing, Lance?" Joe's question surprised him. Lance immediately turned to look at me.

I asked, "Did your testing come out clean? No health problems on the monthly test? Ours are clean."

Lance cleared his throat before saying, "Yes, I'm clean." He concealed the awkwardness by taking another sip of beer.

"IUD inside. No need to bother with condoms, as long as you always use them outside of us."

"Well, I can't lose my job from getting bad results, can I? Of course, I always use them." He took his time while we all knew that he was still trying to process it.

"You can ask them if they mind sharing me." I took another sip of beer, and then I felt Sandy's finger pushing up the bottom of my bottle. I was ordered to finish the entire bottle in front of Lance.

"You see, Lance, if you want us to share Mia with you, then you need to understand one principal thing." Joe started to unbutton my shirt while I kept drinking the beer.

"And what is that?" Lance licked his lips while staring at my exposed lace bra.

I finished my beer as ordered. My shirt was being taken off of me. The button on my trousers was undone, and the zipper followed.

"On duty, she's Captain Phinnisee. But tell him what you are in our room, Mia. Eyes on Lance," said Sandy, grinning at me. The brothers were both touching me at a slow pace for Lance to see.

"Your whore. Mmhh..." While keeping eye contact with Lance, I said, "Please, I need to come. You've been torturing me long enough already."

Sandy continued, "Say, *'Please, Lance.'* Learn to beg him if you want to be his whore, too."

"Look, hold on. I'm not who you think I am. I'm not as nice as when I work. I don't—"

"Good. Welcome to our bed, Lance. Sandy and I have been denying our whore here. It's the second day she's been edged." Joe pulled me by the hair, exposing my neck. "Take off your trousers and pull your knickers to the side. Show Lance how desperate you are to get off."

I did exactly what he commanded, taking my trousers off while sitting. My chest was moving fast up and down. I showed Lance how wet my pussy was. "Please, Lance."

"On all four, Mia. Crawl to me," Lance said, giving me his first command. He put his beer on the table beside him.

Joe whispered in my ear, "Do as he says; we'll watch him from here. We'll see if he gets the balls to use you like his whore. He can't be soft with you."

Sandy rubbed my belly. "And we'll watch you from here, in case you disobey him and aren't being a good whore for him."

I crawled towards Lance, desperately trying to get my release from any of them. Like a pet waiting for his next command, I sat on my knees before him.

Instead of giving commands, he slapped me across the face. He put me on my knees by stretching me up by the throat. "So you've been their whore this whole time, huh?"

He smirked at my nod. "Use your words, Mia. What do you need from me?"

"Please... make me your whore, Lance. This mouth can be yours. These breasts, this pussy, and this arse can be yours, too."

He paused, watching my face closely. "What took you so long?"

"What—what do you mean?" His face was full of unspoken, hidden struggles. I had never seen this version of Lance before. "I, um... I didn't know, Lance. It was only last night that Sandy mentioned something about you."

He turned his face towards Sandy. Lance kept his right hand as my necktie. With Sandy's habit, he must be shrugging his shoulders by now. Lance returned his face to me. "How long have I been sailing beside you?"

"Three and a half years. Lance—"

"That's right. THREE.FUCKING.AND A HALF YEARS. Three and a half years, not to mention a fucking year before that. I was begging them to transfer me to your rotation. Three fucking and a half years fucking around those sluts with similar eyes, a similar smile, similar hair, a similar silly hopping walk, or the similar fucking whatever that could remind me of *you*. I've been chasing your shadow this entire time." His left hand was pointing a finger at nothingness on the wall as he spoke. His words instantly made my tears run like a waterfall.

When I placed my hand on his chest, I could feel his heart beating fast. It was exploding, as my heart was. I wanted to feel this man's heart that he had for me.

Joe and Sandy could be rough with me. But no one had ever yelled at me and outburst the pain the way Lance did. Four and a half years in total was a long period of time. I felt like a fool for not noticing him. I always had him beside me the entire time.

When I started to sob, his pain rushed into my chest, straight to my heart. "I'm sorry, Lance. Please, I thought you were nice to everyone."

He grinned while watching me sob like a child. "No, I'm not nice. Now, take it out and show me how sorry you are."

After taking his cock from his trousers, I carefully circled and licked his tip. I made sure his cock was well cared for while my sobbing didn't stop. Even some of my tears dropped on his length. I tried to keep my breathing as steady as I could in between sobbing and swallowing his cock.

He made a ponytail out of my hair with his fist, guiding my pace. His cock popped out of my mouth when he pulled my hair back. He lifted me from the floor and sat me on his lap.

My bra cups were pulled down. My breasts were being freed for him to slap. My nipples were hurting from his slaps and bites—hurtfully good. I was trying to reach for his cock, but he slapped my hand.

"Don't!" Lance pulled my bra straps down to the sides. After pulling my arms to the back, he slipped both my forearms under the bra wings. He kept making my breasts his toys, as he deserved it.

I begged harder for his mercy to take me. "Please, Lance. It's been too long for the both of us." I felt him growl with my nipple in his mouth.

Lance brought me to bed. His broad shoulders and built up body were fully covered in tattoos. He set my pussy free from my knickers, which made my wetness instantly leak out of me. He shoved my knickers into my mouth before slapping my cheeks and breasts in turns.

My legs stayed spread wide for him to eat my swollen clit. He hugged my thighs to pull me closer to his starving mouth. Drinking my juice. Lapping my neediness.

As I was restrained, my whimpers echoed throughout the bedroom. I could see Sandy and Joe watching as my needs tortured me. They were pumping their cocks with their fists, catching pleasure for themselves.

Lance stripped himself naked. "Once I'm inside you, then you'll become my whore, Mia. There's no going back." He pulled my knickers out of my mouth to hear my consent.

"Please, Lance. You deserve to make me your whore after that long." My pussy was stretched by his thick length in one stroke. "Oh, Lance..."

He was fucking me senseless with his cock while his hand continued to be my necktie. His other hand was free to slap me as he pleased.

"That's it, Mia. You're close. You better come hard like a good whore if you want to be my whore." The way he fucked me sent me straight to seeing stars. By being rough, he freed me. "What a good whore we got here! So obedient."

Sandy approached my mouth while pumping his cock. Joe followed from the other side of my mouth.

"Open wide. Get your tongue out." Lance spat into my mouth, followed by Sandy spraying his cum. Joe followed his brother, filling my mouth with his cum and his spit.

"Swallow if you want me to cum inside this cunt."

I didn't waste any of what they gave me. With three pumps, my pussy was filled with every drop of Lance.

"Lance, I'm sorry. I should have known. I shouldn't have ignored you. I—"

He cupped my face, caring for me. "Shh, Mia, it's all right. I'm right here. I'm always here for you, but now you know the truth. Everything's gonna be all right."

After releasing the bra clips underneath me, he let me hug him tightly. He let me continue sobbing like a child underneath him. This time, I was begging for his forgiveness.

"Hey, hey, hey, listen to me. Look at me. From now on, there will be no other woman. If there is one, these brothers will make sure that I die a slow and painful death. Do you hear me? Just you, Mia."

My sobbing didn't let me speak my 'aye.' I could only nod to Lance. I had never seen him smile like this before.

Joe kissed my temple. "We'll leave you two alone to catch up on some lost time."

Sandy followed by kissing the top of my head. "You're in good hands, baby girl. It's all right."

After the brothers left the room, Lance carried me to the shower. Once both of us were clean, he laid me down properly in bed. With my head resting on his arm, he calmed me down. He cuddled me so gently that I could feel his heart beating for me. "Time to fall into the night, little Polaris."

On a merchant ship, a stranger raised this orphan. All he knew was survival and counting on his strength. From the first day he was sent to my bridge, he always followed my orders. Only today did I find out that he never did. He had been following me all this time. His little Polaris. His North Star. He had been following me to navigate his life.

9

A Covenant

"Good morning, little star." He woke me up with a gentle kiss on my lips. His fingers brushed my tangled morning hair.

"Good morning." I caught him staring at me. "What? Something wrong with me?"

"No, just something right. *Mine.* Your name said so. I might not be Italian, but I know what Mia means. Well, I don't know what I am."

"Didn't you get ancestor tracking tests?"

"Well, I did it only to find out if there was anyone connected. I didn't read the race stuff. Didn't matter. You can read it if you want."

"If it didn't matter to you, then it wouldn't matter to me, either. And I know exactly what you are, Lance. *Mine.*"

"I'm yours, little star. Always have been." He devoured my lips, just like he wasn't letting me go ever again. His kisses moved down to my breasts and my pussy. "Hmm. We taste so good together.

I'm gonna fill you with my cum as many times as I can."

"Yes, please do."

His two fingers massaged my walls with care. "Here's my perfect breakfast. Come for me, little star." A third finger entered my core to stretch me.

"I'm close already. Please, I need your cock to fuck me."

He moved up to kiss my lips. His three fingers kept stretching me, with his thumb circling my clit. "It's our pussy. We do whatever we want with our whore. You don't get to decide. Tell me again what you are."

"Your whore, Lance. Please."

"Come to my hand." No matter how much I begged him, he didn't give his cock to my pussy. He got me off without him inside me. When he pulled his fingers out of me, I became empty once more. He sucked my cum from his fingers, just like he only finished eating and didn't want to leave any taste of the food in his fingers.

"I want more from my whore, but we need to get ready. It's deployment day. I'll be sharing my whore later with Joe and Sandy."

"But I need you now. We still have time. Please."

He growled in my ear. "This whore's trying to be demanding, or what?" He rolled me to the side. With my head resting on his arm, he held me tight against his chest. He was long and thick in the best way possible, and he used me the way it fit him.

My existence was full of him; this moment was all about him. His embrace spooned me tightly. His strokes woke me up roughly from behind. After years of being blind, I became fully awakened from the inside out. What I did to him was wrong, but he did me right. Roughly; he did me roughly so he got my full attention.

"You're trying to be a brat now? Hmm? This is what a brat gets. But we punish a brat and a whore the same way." His fingers started circling and rubbing my clit mercilessly. "I said I wanted more from my whore."

"Oh, Lance—"

"Feel what you did to me. Fuck, I'm close already. My whore better come now." He came right after my second release. Then he scooped up our cum. "Open your mouth. That's how good we are together, little star."

He showered me and washed my hair after our morning fuck. Pouring me with kisses. Showering me with care. I need this. We need this.

After that, it was my turn to caress him. I cooked a real edible breakfast for us. Those green eyes followed my every move in the kitchenette.

"Mmh... Trust me, it's better than Amma's cooking." It was simply scrambled eggs and cheese toasties that he was talking about.

"I added more cheese to it. So you won't need to get cheesy today."

"Let's not forget the entire block of cheese grated on top of the toast. Look at that golden, melting cheese. You're gonna make me fat, little star."

While he was chewing a mouthful of it, I kissed him generously. "Well, I can help you with the *cardio* at any time in case you gain some weight."

We finished our breakfast and got ready to start our day. We were to help prepare the shadow-workers for deployment. Joe and Sandy were already there, along with the health personnel and equipment crew members.

Amma gasped when we walked towards her. "Lance, are you all right? Have you gone mental? A smile in the morning?" She placed the back of her hand on his forehead, just like a mum checking if her son had a fever.

"She cooked some breakfast for me, Amma." Immediately, he got a slap on the back of his head.

"I've run out of nieces and friends' daughters to try matching you with anyone. If only you didn't wander around like some rascals with girls from wherever, you could have saved years in your life.

She's always been on the same bridge with you the entire time."

"Aih, Amma... Can you stop embarrassing me for once?"

"Oh, you one ungrateful child. I'm supposed to embarrass you for the rest of your life. You just wait until Appa Zhou reincarnates near you, so he can smack you in the head."

Amma was the closest thing to a mother that Lance had. I didn't know that *Amma* means 'mother.' She sort of raised him because she used to work on the same merchant ship as the sailor who found him. They called the sailor *Appa*, which means 'father.' Their crew raised him in some way, since Lance was found.

Because of her time on the merchant ship, she became a logistician on Slava. She handled inventories, keeping records of them. "You two grew up with the captain, yes?"

Joe and Sandy nodded to her while painfully holding back their laughter.

"Good. If this rascal ever hurts her, you torture him before you kill him, yes? Don't make it quick! Make it the longest death that you can stretch out of his life."

"Ugh, I already told them that last night," Lance said while massaging his head. He could have me massaging his other head later on.

To the Ceolmund brothers, she said, "Good. A covenant it is."

Lance and Amma used to be in the same duty rotation before Lance was transferred to mine. I found out that when he asked for a transfer, he told the institution that he wouldn't be able to watch Amma when he was on active duty. As a result, he became a reserve crew member on her rotation. Whenever she was on duty, he was always on board until her rotation was completed. Amma's rotation would end in Freemantle, but she would continue to sail with us until we ported in Bali. She said that she wanted to visit the temples.

***

All shadow-workers needed to undergo health assessments twice on deployment day; two hours after breakfast and two hours after lunch. After passing the morning assessment, the equipment crew prepared weaponry for them to check.

If they passed the afternoon assessment, the ship crews prepared the wardrobes according to each assignment. The shadow-workers didn't bring anything but their weapons of choice under their clothes. They used blue dry suits and diving equipment when offboarding Slava.

When approaching sunset, the deck crew blew the horn, giving signals. Guests would gather to enjoy their last sunset on the ship. While those guests were so focused in one direction, we opened the door on Deck 1, opposite the sunset. Whether it was starboard or port, it depended on the bearing of the ship.

Shadow-workers were to be deployed using the door that we used to move out the rubbish when porting. Because of the nature of our operation, our regular porting schedule was around seven to eight in the evening. Of course, with some exceptions for several routes. However, since we had the situation at Australia's headquarters, our schedules were adjusted. We would set sail early in the morning after getting everything we needed for the journey.

10

Harbouring

We were on high alert. We would be 250 shadow-workers lighter when we ported to Melbourne. All the remaining shadow-workers on board and the deck crews were carrying a weapon—well, at least one. Lance was carrying as well, since he was a reserved crew member.

"My goodness, this woman." Lance sighed when he noticed Amma approaching. "Amma, what the hell are you doing here? The door's still open. You get back to your suite."

"What an ungrateful rascal this one is. Here, I made some dosa for the four of you. You haven't eaten, have you? Your key?"

"Just keep the door unlocked. Like anyone would steal your dosa from smelling it across the aisle." Lance gave her the key to his quarter. He chuckled and shook his head. "Thank you, Amma."

Sandy asked in a whisper, "Hey, just to be clear here, we share Mia with you, yes?"

"Yeah, what about it?"

"Do you mind sharing Amma with me? I mean, her cooking looks much tastier than Joe's, *that I can tell.*" He left us to follow Amma's food.

"Unbelievable." Lance shook his head before leaving me and Joe to help monitor the door.

Sandy was already eating the dosa when Joe and I finally found Lance's quarter. "Mmh... Way better than your cooking, Joe."

"And you didn't even wait for him. You just dug in. What is it with this sprog?"

I heard Lance coming in. "So, this is where you sleep. No wonder we didn't realise you were on board."

He smiled at me, though I knew that there was much I didn't realise about him. "This was Amma's. What was I supposed to do? Letting her sleep in a quarter like this? Better to switch her to my suite so she has a kitchen to cook in. Besides, it isn't that bad."

"Finish eating, Sandy?"

"Yup. Finished. Oh, it was so good."

"Great. Now you get eaten first," said Lance. He pulled me by the hair and whispered, "Our whore must be starving. Go get your meat and swallow him."

As commanded, I moved down from Lance's bed to crawl towards Sandy. I took his cock out and started licking his tip.

Suddenly, my hair was pulled back again. "Lance said to swallow it, Mia. Then obey him and swallow Sandy's," Joe said.

My other two men were stripping me down while I was swallowing Sandy. My body became their toy to touch, squeeze, and pinch. It was that easy for them to command my pussy to betray me. My arousal started to pool in my knickers.

Joe massaged my arse while he took out his cock and thrust into me. Slowly, until he wasn't.

Both of their cocks were out of me. Sandy pulled down his trousers and said, "Sit on my lap facing him." Sandy's cock filled me first. After leaning back against his chest, my pussy received another cock.

"I'm full. Plea—" Then Lance shut my mouth up with his cock.

"This quarter isn't like the suite. Everyone can hear you here, little star."

Joe said, "He better shut you up with his cock for good. We can't let anyone hear your moan."

Lance thrust into my throat as he shut me up. When he gagged me, my tunnel clenched the brothers. They went faster, as if catching my release so that no one would hear. "Come, now, little fish. Drown us with your cum."

Even with Lance filling my mouth, I couldn't hold back the whimper as I came. Sandy followed my release, filling me with his warmth.

Lance pulled out his cock to slap my face. "What did I say about being silent?" It was his slap that sent Joe to his release.

After the brothers pulled themselves out of me, Lance pulled me by the waist. On the edge of his bed, he planted himself up to my hilt. This position exposed both of us for the brothers to watch. By lifting my thighs up and wide, he reached me deeply.

Joe covered my mouth with his hands while Sandy was circling my overly sensitive clit.

"What a show you two give us here," said Joe.

Then I reached my second release while being shut into silence. It felt so good to be hugged tightly from behind when Lance reached his release.

Joe freed my mouth from his hand. "That's our good, obedient whore." With his kisses, he wiped my tears away.

Sandy fed me the mixture of our releases. "The four of us must taste better than three."

"Uh, huh. The best taste I could ever have. I want more of us like this."

Lance whispered in my ear, "After Sandy finishes feeding you, clean up all your mess with your mouth. Be a good slave for us, not just a whore."

"Ugh, you heard him, Mia? He wants to make you our slave, too. Good thing we share you with him." One by one, I licked my men clean. They left me with Lance afterwards.

"You need to eat, little star. Come on, tomorrow's gonna be a long day. After this, you can go to sleep. Promise, I'll snuggle you 'til there's no more stars tonight. I'll still be here when morning comes."

"Okay... Okay."

As much as I needed to eat, all I wanted was to crawl into his arms. Lance didn't let me; instead, he fed me in his bed. He didn't stop kissing me after each bite, either. "That's my good little star."

11

Fishing Day

Lance's kisses woke me up in the morning. He was already fully clothed when he started to have his breakfast—me. Every part of my pussy was well eaten, and every drop of my juice was lapped up. He made time to give me a release before he left for the fishing day.

With his gun in the holster, he was set to be on call for active duty in case something happened or if a crew needed to be replaced. He took a quick look at his uniform in the mirror. He didn't wear any stripes or neckties today. We used them only when we were the active crew. Through the reflection, he caught me while I was capturing the view of his features in my mind. He winked at me before getting out of the quarter.

Beacons were off at dawn for the loadings to be able to find us. Slava set sail at 7:30 a.m. standard time. The new guests were led to the restaurant to have their first breakfast on board.

Their next schedule included facility tours with the designated guide crews. The remaining guests from the previous trip were required to join because there were safety briefings integrated into the tour. This way, the ship crew could easily guide the guests away from the direction of the fishing.

Deployments were much easier than fishing. Today, both forward and aft doors on both sides of Deck 1 were operational. Nets were thrown through those doors to catch about 200 shadow-workers diving in the sea. Before we pulled the nets, we placed a railing at each door—one end was locked at the top aft and the other at the middle bottom. By having these, we maintained the tension and pressure balance when pulling the nets.

We threw and pulled the nets in turns so we wouldn't miss any shadow-workers, especially the injured ones. Those shadow-workers were the loadings that we needed to fish out of the sea.

The first pull had always been the hardest since my first sailing time on Slava—it was to fish the injured ones. Even if those shadow-workers, shoulder-to-shoulder helped each other accomplish projects, someone might get hurt in the process. This situation in Australia was not excluded.

The ship crews and shadow-workers on board were ready for the pull from the opening doors to the aisle through the medical centre. The first pull was from the forward door, then from the aft door.

Only ship crews were allowed to help with the first pull, while the shadow-workers were guarding. We carried them to the wet room, away from the cargo haul. It was where the mess happened. In that room, we stripped them out of their dry suits. Right there, immediately, we could see how bad they were, from bullet wounds and open cuts to blast injuries. Medical personnel separated them by the degree of their injuries. The injured were triaged before being moved to the next room, either the operation room or the hall of the medical centre.

Sometimes, it wasn't the physical that became heavy for me; instead, it was the rush of emotions from what I saw. The first one was a bullet wound that didn't pass through. Because I didn't have any licences, I couldn't help with any procedures. I was only to carry around their supplies, equipment, or tools if they needed something far away from them.

From the bullet wound, we moved on to the next one, blade cuts. He lost lots of blood reaching here. Not because it was a big cut, but because there were several of them. He taped those cuts, mostly with duct tape. The bigger cut had a menstrual pad underneath the tape. I was almost laughing when I saw it. When he saw my shocked expression, he began to laugh, which helped free me from feeling bad. He said that it worked well, and today I learnt something new.

The next one was another bullet wound injury. All of the bullets passed through her, then she shoved the bleeding from some of those wounds shut with tampons. I was helping to dress one of her wounds when a shadow-worker abruptly pulled me out.

"Hey, what the fuck? Hands of me!"

"Yeah, good luck with that. The question is, Captain, what the fuck are you down here?" He brought me around and up. We were constantly walking until we reached and entered a suite. "Clean yourself, Captain."

"Hey, no need to be so rough."

"Huh, surely you like rough if you're dealing with him."

With him grinning, it made me want to punch him so badly. But then I saw one of my men. "Lance, aren't you supposed to be moving around? Don't touch me. I'm a mess here."

"I *am* moving around. The bathroom's empty. Right there if you want to clean up." He showed me the way and gave me some time to catch my breath.

I was refreshing my face in the bathroom when I heard Joe and Sandy outside. Their voices sounded so familiar that they reminded me of home. I wondered why we were brought here all of a sudden. Was the situation that bad?

"Mia? You okay?"

"Yeah, I'm all right, Sandy."

Joe asked the shadow-workers who brought us here, "Mind telling us the situation? Why are we here?"

"We're in lockdown—suites and offices," she said. "Captain, your suite is on the forward eighth, correct?"

"Correct. Should I return there?"

"No. You should be moving hourly."

"Older Ceolmund on the aft sixth, younger on the forward seventh, and Zhou on the forward ninth, correct?"

"No, I'm on forward five."

"Why are you in a crew quarter? You're assigned to forward nine."

"Mum's a logistician. What? Oh, am I supposed to be scared of you, lady? Just wait until you see her with a flip flop in her hand. She'd kill me first for letting her sleep in a quarter on Deck 5."

"Fine. But all of you need to keep moving until we're off the lockdown."

"I can go to Joe's suite at lunch and mine at supper. Probably with Amma at midnight. Joe can go to mine, Sandy's, and yours. Sandy, go to yours, Jo's, and mine. Lance, I can't know where you go."

"And I'll go around," said Lance. He could not tell any of us where he was. As a reserve, he could only tell the active top four in command. "Oh, don't forget to get your lunch at Amma's. She cooked chicken biryani for us. I just had mine."

12

Fixing the Catch

All four of us decided to put a set of clean clothes in each other's rooms during fishing day. We wouldn't know how long this operation lasts. In case we needed a fuck in between, clean clothes would be available right away.

Even if it was only half past noon, I was already much in need of a shower. I walked out of the common room, following Joe to his suite. We showered together, Joe and I. It was going to be a quick shower, but I wasn't sure about a quick fuck.

"What's the matter, little fish? Did Lance get you off this morning?"

"He did, but he didn't give me his cock. He just sprayed his cum on me. Joe, please."

"Awesome. He marked you, then. Spread your legs." He found the wetness pooling in my folds. "Oh, our pussy is always needy." While he was pinning me to the bathroom wall, his finger thrust in and out of me.

"Hmm... Another one, please."

"That's it. My little fish's clenching tightly. Let me be generous once in a while." His thumb played with my clit while the other two fingers were curling inside me. "You like that? Hmm? Do you like me being generous like this?"

"Mmm...hmm. Oh, I like that. It feels so good. Please don't stop." He pulled my wrist when I was reaching for his cock. He pinned it above my head.

"This whore's so needy for cocks. You're *our* whore. Remember that. You don't get to ask. You take whatever we give you."

"Please, Joe. I'm close." I was given a third finger inside me. I was stretched and desperate for his cock.

"Ugh, we like our whore this way, begging."

"Joe, I'm gonn—mmh...please, I need your cock fucking me hard. Imma—" My second orgasm of the day rushed in. The moans echoed off the bathroom tiles. No cock had filled me today. Here I was, coming onto his hand.

He scooped all the cum from my folds. All of it was now spread all over my face. "Now you smell like our pussy. On your knees."

With me kneeling before him, he started pumping his cock with his fist. I watched as he kept pumping his thickness. As I was craving him, I parted my lips and stuck out my tongue.

"Look at this good whore kneeling and begging. So beautiful. You want my cock?"

"Please... mercy."

"Because you beg nicely, I give you mercy. Close your eyes, little fish."

Desperate—that was how I became. I felt the warmth of him hitting my face. I opened my eyes to his grin before he spat into my mouth and on my face.

"My good little fish. Now, clean yourself up before getting your lunch." He left me there in the bathroom, on my knees, with so much humiliation. After I finished cleaning up, I went to have my lunch.

***

She opened the door for me with warmth. "Mia, come in. Joe's eating already. We were talking about you three and your father."

"Which part? There are some very interesting ones he might not tell."

"Oh, we were only in the beginning. Now I'm curious."

I chuckled as I took my seat. "Did he tell you why my father only took Sandy with us and left him behind?"

"Ugh, my first heartbreak. Three of them left me alone and set sail. That's why Sandy has a higher rank, Amma, because he started his training much earlier than me."

"Why did her father leave you? What did you do?" Amma gave him an interrogating look.

"Well, her father told me and Sandy to make a net and left the two of us alone. And then ships started coming in, like lots of them. Imagine a teenager seeing different types of ships with different colours and different people coming out of them. That was what I always wanted."

"So, he left Sandy to make the net alone while he went to watch the ships. Sandy was smaller than him at the time, making a big net by himself. Can you imagine that?"

"I was thirteen at that time, and Sandy was ten. So I drew those ships with charcoal. Our parents didn't get much money to buy colour pencils."

"When my father returned, he smacked his head with the drawing book. He said that Sandy was good at following orders. It turned out that my father was right that Joe has always had a better view from afar."

"It still hurts, though. He brought my drawings, but not me."

Amma asked, "Did he give them back to you?"

"He *did*, actually, before he passed away."

"So, he *did* leave you behind on purpose." Joe and I looked at each other in confusion at her words. "Look, I've known seafarers much longer than you have, kids. Her father must have thought that either you'd be good at doing something else or you'd need to learn something else first before joining him. It could be both. Where did you go after they left?"

"A few shadow-workers took me under their wings. They weren't shadow-workers yet at that time. They were hidden, seeking refuge in the forest. Their leader became a language teacher, hiding their identity. Now his son has become their new leader. Do you know the Watchman in the archive?"

"Oh, you mean the motorcyclist Bratva? You were with them? I've never talked to any of them. Not that they're scary, but more likely intimidating."

"They're not that scary once you know them. They just don't smile that much. I was with them for about five years until her father returned with Sandy and Mia."

"And for the safety crew, you need to see everything with a broader view to see everything as a whole. You can't really do that unless you have eaten the high and low in life." Amma shook her head and laughed at Joe. "So, her father *was right* all along."

"If you put it that way, he was," Joe said.

13

Damage Control

He pulled my trousers down along with my knickers. Sandy bent me over the dining table on my stomach, readying me for him to come home. "Legs, wide. I want to play with my food."

Only by those words was I wet for him already. It was exposed and flooded in front of him. With a whining voice, I begged him. "Lance and Joe got me off, but I haven't given any cock today, Sandy."

He sat down, facing his meal—my wet pussy. He massaged my thighs and up to my arse. "Good for you. You sometimes forget that *this* is ours. We get to choose what to give you and *when* to give you anything." He parted my folds for him to lick my neediness.

"Mmh... please, Sandy, have mercy on me. I've been empty the entire day."

Then his slap landed on my arse, and then another one followed. He kept lapping my arousal, not caring about my desperation. For him, it was simply his appetiser before tea. He was drinking my wetness only to satisfy his thirst. "Lay on your back. Spread open for me."

With my back lying on the table, I put my heels at the edge to spread my legs wider. With my fingers, I spread open my fold, begging for his cock. "Please, Sandy, your pussy needs to be filled."

He slapped me. "What a beautiful cunt we have here. Always needy, easily gets drenched." He took his cock out and stroked it with his fist. So close, yet so unreachable for me to have it.

"Only the good whore gets a reward." His tongue started to fill my needy hole. Fucking it, lapping it wildly, and sucking it hard. A forced orgasm—that was what he gave me. He showered my belly with the warmth of his release. "Don't clean yourself. I want everyone to smell my cum on you."

We left my suite for tea at the restaurant. Sandy ate on a different deck, far away from me. I saw none of my two other mates here. I needed them at a time like this.

Everyone was quiet. They came to eat, finished their food quickly, and then left. Some of them took their food to go. We were scheduled to port in Adelaide the day after tomorrow. So the logisticians were occupied with calculating and preparing for the next fishing day.

Other than the reserved crew, it was unusual for me to be pulled out of the fishing day. There must be some serious situations going on on the ground. No one was giving me any clear information about it.

From the restaurant on Deck 8, I went straight up. I needed to have a word with the captain. When he saw me approaching the bridge, he walked out of it and closed the door behind him.

"My duty rotation will start in Freemantle. I need at least a heads up about the situation. How bad is it, Captain?"

"Not now, Captain. After Adelaide, we can talk. We're in lockdown until the next fishing day is finished."

"At least tell me about the loadings and logistics."

He sighed and put his hands on his waist. "There were 231 loadings, but 22 did not make it. That's all I can tell for now."

"And the rest of my crew?"

"They won't be able to reach Adelaide, so we port in Albany to board them."

"All right, then. We talk after Adelaide."

"Captain, please don't get me wrong. I can't tell you about anything that I don't already get from the higher chain."

"I'd do the same thing."

After excusing myself from the active captain, I decided to return to my suite. I felt like I was in limbo for these entire situations at work. Also, I felt some damage as a result of my men's rejection.

Once I was in my suite, I found Sandy lying in bed. He was here as planned; I wasn't. He rose from the bed to embrace me, but I went straight to take a shower. I neither asked nor said anything to him.

While washing my hair, I felt his hands rubbing my back. He joined me inside. He lathered me with soap, giving me a shoulder and neck massage. "You were supposed to be staying with Amma, not here. What is it, baby girl? You're tense. You want to talk about it?"

"No."

He smiled at his brat—me. "Let's get you clean and dry before bed." He dried my hair with a hairdryer while I was brushing my teeth after our shower. None of us were saying anything. He understood me whenever I was like this.

When I finally rested my head on the pillow, my mouth was silent, although my brain was loud. Even with my eyes closed, I could feel him watching me. He was in full attention when I opened my eyes; his temple rested on his fist. His other hand gently rubbed my belly, moving lower to where my womb sat. Sometimes I wondered if he ever wanted a child with me. He'd be a fun, playful, and protective father one day.

After sliding his arm underneath my neck, I snuggled in his warm hug. My waist was pulled closer to him as if I were weightless in his arm. "I like being hugged like this."

"I like hugging you like this, too. This way, I can make sure that you're mine."

"Good night, Sandy. Thank you for today."

"Not even the Kraken can bother you in your sleep." He was drowning me in his warm kisses. My body sank under his cradle.

"Hmm."

"Dream of me, baby girl. I'll be right here when you open your eyes in the morning. Then you'll realise that I'm no longer a dream."

14

Red Flagged

His kisses woke me up in the morning. He stroked me from behind; this time he was gentle with me. "Owh, my baby girl's bleeding this morning."

"Mmh... What do I owe this favour?"

"Nothing, baby girl. You owe me nothing. So this was why you went to bed upset last night. Was it the PMS or the fact that none of us were giving you any of our cocks?"

"Probably both." I was indeed upset about my tunnel being kept empty. "You said that you made me your whore, but none of your cocks used me yesterday."

"But our whore is also our toy to play with." He thrust me while talking dirty in my ear. "We like watching how bad you want us. But it's also satisfying to watch you shower us with your cum."

"I also like how badly you treat your whore. You make me feel... mmh, useful. You give me purpose. I'm supposed to be useful for the three of you."

He kissed my face, down to my neck and shoulder. His gentle hand squeezed my breasts and pinched my nipples. "I agree. We should use our whore hardly. Treat her badly until she can do nothing but beg for more." He loved to give me a necktie with his hand when controlling me. His thrust became harder, fucking my pussy like a property he owned.

"Sandy... Hhh..."

"Our whore should be coming when we tell you to come. Are you being our good whore, Mia?"

"Yes. Oh, yes, I'm close. Harder, please. Fuck me harder, like you don't care if your whore gets hurt. Fuck me like you hate me commanding you around the bridge."

He growled in my ear. "Come. Now. Show your owner how good of a whore you are." Both of his hands were around my neck, giving him something to hold on to.

My pussy was pooled with a mix of my wetness and blood. Maybe I was supposed to be their sex slave instead of their whore. Being fucked by his harder thrust like this proved it. Just like he commanded me to, I let myself go.

"That's my good whore. You let us use you like a toy. That's our reward for following you as our captain."

The mixture of my cum and blood was now added with the warmth of his cum. My bedsheet was a mess with evidence of our passion.

"Orgasm can help with your cramps, baby girl. Let me shower you again before we have breakfast, yes?"

"You always know me well. I like that about you, Sandy."

After a bloody fuck, a poached egg and toast were all I could have. I didn't feel like eating a heavy breakfast this morning. Sandy had gone to the gym, though it was later than usual. We were to keep moving and changing our routines, especially Lance.

"Can I have a briefing with my crew daily?"

"It's too dangerous to put all four of you together in a room."

"There must be some vacant saferoom that we can use. My rotation starts in Freemantle. At least we have briefings before starting our duties, unless you find anyone who can brief me about our situation in detail," I said firmly to the timekeeper. They functioned as schedulers for the institution.

"Is it the way of saying that you want a place for your mates to fuck your every hole at the same time? I can't help you set up briefings."

"What did you say?"

"That's why we are *that* good at doing our job." He smirked at me, glorifying his winning argument. "However, let's pretend that we don't know about the *'sharing is caring'* between the four of you. Let me ask the higher-ups what I can do to help prepare you for duty."

"We'd appreciate that." I left the timekeeper's office without changing my walking pace. So here we had the institution red-flagged us.

Before exiting the office, I bumped into a shadow-worker. "Shouldn't you be carrying, Captain?"

"I haven't been briefed. Do you mind telling me anything that is allowed and can be useful for me?"

"No, I don't mind, Captain. 'You should be carrying.' That can be useful, innit?" That was all he said to me. That one sentence led me to the shop department.

Our shop had two functions, one of which was for guests to buy their clothing and accessories. The other was for shadow-workers and crew members to pick up suits and small weapons.

I took a knife and a small handgun with me. I kept moving hourly for the rest of the day. Moving from one point to another until the end of the day. I missed my men so much the entire day. When

tucking myself into bed alone tonight, I imagined
how I'd be waking up alone in the morning.

90

15

Sinking In

The horn woke me up in the morning. We must had ported to Adelaide at dawn. I began to have cramps after preparing breakfast for myself. All I could think about was cuddling with my men. If only we didn't have to keep moving and missing each other like this.

"Damn this lockdown. And damn those motherfuckers seeking war with the institution!"

Common people might see us as loading logistics and unloading waste. What we unloaded was actually something that wasn't worth the time and energy to process. Among that rubbish, there were things that we caught in our nets on fishing days. While catching the shadow-workers, much more interesting things got caught as well. Sometimes I wondered how stuffed animals, furniture, household items, and even electronics could even be in the sea.

Slava had her own holistic waste management system. We made our fertiliser from organic and animal waste. Those fertilisers helped grow our fruit and vegetables in the greenhouses and on our onboard farm on Deck 13. We sailed at 7:45 this morning for another fishing day as I continued my hourly movement.

After lunch, I went to the kitchen to get some chocolate because my cramps were getting worse. One of the chefs made me a traditional drink made of curcuma, kaempferiae galanga, ginger, pandanus screwpine, cinnamon, and tamarind. He wrote me all the ingredients and the recipe as well. He was used to making that drink for his sister and wife in the place where he came from. He made a bottle for me to take. Sandy was right—orgasm helped with my cramps yesterday. But not today.

The mood for exercising wasn't quite there, but I needed to keep my head straight by myself. So I did some yoga in the afternoon to keep myself grounded, even with the waves of the sea. My stomach was bloating, but not because of seasickness.

Nothing. I heard nothing about the fishing day or the situation on the ground. I didn't think pushing the active captain would do any good with my current mood. He would give us briefings if there was any further confirmed information. Everything was still unclear.

In the evening, Amma cooked yellow rice and chicken curry for tea. It smelt so fragrant with the spices she used. Asian traditional dishes were famous for using spices. It tasted good, so I couldn't waste it, even with my bloating stomach.

Lance came into the suite when I was eating. He hugged me tightly, showering me with kisses in front of Amma. "Owh, my little star's getting sick today, yes?"

"Um, just cramps." I buried my face in his chest, inhaling the scent that I'd been missing.

He sat me on his lap and cupped my jaw. "Thank you for taking care of her, Amma."

Amma put his food on a plate and placed it near mine. "Don't forget to eat. I'll leave you two alone. I don't need to witness too much from these lovebirds."

Once Amma left us, Lance turned his face towards me. "I can't wait to fill you with my baby. You won't have to deal with cramps like this for at least nine months."

I chuckled at his words. "We've only been together for less than a week. Honestly, baby talk already?"

"I've been with you long enough, little star." He rubbed my belly, saying, "*This* will be swollen one day. And I'll keep fucking you until you give birth to my baby."

"Will you still be fucking me when I get fat like a whale?"

"Of course I will. Mummy whale's carrying my baby whale." He fed me a spoonful of the yellow rice. "Come on now, finish your food."

"You, too, need to eat." I brushed his hair with my fingers. "Um, Lance."

"Yes, little star?"

"Can we watch a film after this?"

"Of course we can. I'd love to go on a date with you." He kissed me long and gently. "Finish your food first. No but. No excuses."

"All right. All right. Such commanding."

"You're only in command when you're an active captain. Outside the bridge..." He whispered, "We're the ones commanding this body. Three of us will keep fucking you even when you're pregnant with my baby whale."

By his words, my moan slipped out, even though I knew Amma was in the room next to us. I wanted those words to be our reality one day.

We went on our first date to the cinema; many more dates were yet to come. We were supposed to spend the rest of our night together watching a film, but I was drowning in his scent and the comfort of his arms.

I was half asleep when Lance carried me out of the cinema. He laid me in bed and spooned me the entire night. He let me sink into my own starry night sky.

16

Breakfast Time

Lance changed his gym routines with Joe and Sandy during the lockdown. Once I finally woke up, I made a cup of builder for myself.

The kitchenette was almost empty when I checked it. I hadn't asked for restocking from the pantry for quite some time. Some eggs in the refrigerator should be enough to make pancakes for us. After preparing our breakfast, I took a shower. I didn't hear him coming in.

"Hmm, my breakfast looks tasty." He joined me in the shower and started devouring my lips.

"I don't know your favourite topping for pancakes. And I haven't restocked for days."

"My cum, that's my favourite topping for *this* cake," he said while squeezing my arse—his cake. "One day I'm gonna take this hole. I'll make this cake mine."

He kissed me gently and softly, but I knew that he'd been holding himself back. "I got you, little star. I'll fuck you 'til you come, so you won't have cramps today."

"Mmh, Lance, if I knew how badly you'd treat me, I would have begged to be your whore much sooner. You've waited for me too long."

"And how would you offer me for my waiting time? Hmm? Four and a half years of what, Mia?" He reached for my clit to play with it.

"Four and a ha—" I paused to feel his fingers entering me one by one. He gave me two to massage my inner walls. "Four and a half years of discipline as a usable sex slave."

"And I can use my sex slave however I want? Nothing off limits? That sounds tempting. What if I say no?"

My tears started leaking out of my eyes, as did my arousal from my pussy. "Please, Lance. I can be a whore for Joe and Sandy. You've been nice to me all these times. But you don't need to be nice to me if you make me your sex slave."

"Tell me to stop. Or I'll fuck you and use you, just like a slave."

I shook my head.

He slapped me across the face. By the throat, he pinned me to the bathroom wall. "Don't be a fool.

A slave is only the property of its owner. Please tell me to stop, Mia. Because I can't."

While whimpering, I said, "Please don't stop, Lance. Ever. You're my owner now. I'm yours."

He growled, biting my ear. "Then I'll use anything that comes to mind. My fingers, my tongue, my cock, toys, things, even your other men, only to punish you. Then you'll beg me to use you worse than I already did."

"Oh, Lance... yes."

His massage became feral, no longer caring but simply fulfilling his hunger. "Then give me your fucking orgasm. It's for me. Mine. When I ask what's mine, my slave serves it to me." With three fingers inside my hole, he added his thumb to circle my clit. He was in command of my body, demanding that I obey him.

"That's my good whore becoming my sex slave," he said after I came into his hand. He turned me around, facing the bathroom wall.

"Lance..." I widened my stance for him.

He took me from behind while cupping my breasts. With his cock pumping in and out of me, he sank himself into me.

"Come for me again. You're nearly there. Give me one more." His hand reached around for my clit. Those fingers were rubbing me so good.

"Mmh... Lance, I'm—ooh." Releasing for him once again, my pussy clenched on his harder strokes.

"You hug my cock so tight when you come." He stroked me a few more times before pulling out. His release sprayed all over my arse. "That's my perfect breakfast from my perfect slave. What a chewy cake I got here!"

"Oh, Lance, we can't stay in bed today, can we?"

"That's all I wanted to do with you, if only we could." He cupped my jaw and gave me kisses all over my face. "Let me shower you, and then we'll have breakfast together. Okay, little star?"

He caressed me—not only my body but also my heart. Every bite he fed me filled my soul. "I like how you feed me."

"Ugh, I like feeding you, especially with *this*," he said while pointing to his cock.

"Well, Amma can blame herself for not cooking any meat. So, I try to get my meat from her son. I.love.it."

He tucked my hair behind my ears. "To you, I set my course to sail. Always have been. I'll sail through every ocean, sea, and river for my love. I'll build my own raft if I have to, little star. You're the Polaris I navigate my life with."

"Oh, fuck! That's way sexier than him saying, 'I love you,' for sure." His words left me undone. "Lance, I—"

"Shh... You don't need to say anything back. I just need you to know my feelings. And please, stop feeling bad about yourself. It was me, not you. I didn't make a move. I was a coward, Mia."

"But you aren't, Lance. You've done things that other crews didn't have the balls to do. I know that some of them got transferred because they couldn't keep up with me. I've heard things behind my back. I'm a lot to handle sometimes. I know that."

He chuckled. "Yeah, I've got balls. You've been emptying them since we got together. But I agree that you're a *lot* to handle. It takes three to manhandle you properly."

"Do you, in some way, feel jealous about them?"

"No, I'm kind of grateful for them. As you said, you've got a lot to handle. Hey, your words, not mine."

We ate our breakfast together before leaving my suite and going in separate directions. We continued to move around during the day.

I visited the greenhouses in the afternoon. It helped me with my mood to be around plants and the animals we had on board. Helping the crew feed the animals calmed me down, of course, aside from Lance having me as his breakfast.

Being alone with the animals and seeing them with their minis got me thinking about what Lance said to me. I wanted to have children one day. With those three men, would I be giving myself just to any of them if I had a child from one of them? When Lance told me that he loved me, I wondered how I felt about him. I'd love to have his child as much as he would. Would I love him as much as he loves me? He had held his feelings towards me for years.

17

On Call

After waking up the next day at dawn alone in my suite, I immediately took a shower. We were still porting in Albany and hadn't set sail yet. I walked straight towards the bridge to meet with the active captain. We had a deal to talk about the situation after Adelaide.

I knocked on the entrance to the bridge. "I need to have a word with the captain." I was standing outside, but I could see him handing over the command to his second mate.

He walked towards me and closed the door behind him. "Walk with me, Captain. Have you eaten breakfast yet?"

"Can we have a briefing first, then I'll be enjoying my breakfast?"

"You shouldn't skip any meals."

From where we were heading, I knew that it was towards the restaurant on Deck 12. "Can we talk now, Captain?"

"What have you heard so far?"

"So far? Nothing. No one is sharing nothing with me." I got a plate of scrambled eggs and beans.

He put some toast, sunny side up, and bacon on his plate. "Are you carrying?"

"Yes, I passed by a shadow-worker who told me that I should. Care to fill me in on what it meant?"

"I agree about that one." We sat on the outside of the restaurant.

"Elaborate."

"We got 547 loadings from two fishing days. Another one in a few hours." He made a sandwich on his plate while continuing the briefing. "I need you and your crew on call. We *are* the target."

I tried to act normal, pretending to have my usual breakfast briefing. "For what?" I kept eating my food while waiting for his answers.

"You know about the situation in the Northeast, yes?" He took a bite of his sandwich, recognising my head nodding. "They want what's in her belly. Would you give her away for 15 million pounds?"

For sure, my face was giving him a straight, deadly look. What the fuck made him think that I would sell my life, not to mention my men, to anyone for that price? It had quite a lot of zeros, though. So I could imagine the temptation for anyone needy enough or greedy enough.

"Glad to know on which side you're standing, Captain. Act like you know nothing. Keep on moving every hour, for your safety."

"I'll keep moving."

"One more thing before I go. You might want to keep an eye on the orphan."

If only my eyes could kill, they'd be murdering the active captain straight through his eyes and further into his skull.

"He was raised on a merchant ship. But she wasn't always doing business, or so I heard. Only merchants who carried logistics could cross the enemy lines, sometimes."

While holding myself back from punching him in the face, I asked, "And how is that relevant?"

"I'm not sure if he's a trained shadow-worker, but he's been brought up in a grey world since he was little. It could have been something he considered normal." He paused. "And I know that he's never been able to keep his eyes away from you for years. He used to be on my rotation, in case you forgot. He requested a transfer for you."

"Did he tell you all that?"

"No, he didn't. But when he was in my crew rotation, he always made time to contact the younger Ceolmund. Well, he told me that they had been close since their training days. But it wasn't that, was it?"

"All right."

He was making a confused, frowning face. "How do you mean by 'all right,' Captain?"

I gave him nothing but my evil grin.

"As I said at the gym, you and Milady are much alike, unreadable, and up for the long game." He took his time, trying to read me. "Also, just like I said, you two could be quite intimidating."

"Are you intimidated, Captain?"

"I'm all right."

"No, you aren't. You are blushing."

I kept eating slowly, even after the captain left the table. Trying to keep acting as usual, I took some sweets. It was quite tasty, actually.

I even talked to the chef, who made me the traditional drink for my cramps. He deserved the credit, for it helped a lot during my period. Then I left the restaurant to search for my men.

They changed their gym sessions with one another. Lance must had been on the move since we were in the port, so I assumed I'd find Joe at the gym. I assumed, but I could be wrong now and then. This time, my assumption proved that I was indeed wrong.

"Either libraries or bookshops. If I'm missing, you might find the curious Joe anchored to the world inside a book."

I remembered what Joe said a few years ago. While going to our mini library that The Great One opened for his wife, I kept my walking pace steady. It was a mini for him, but surely a massive one for the rest of us.

Any guests and shadow-workers could visit any place on Deck 13 down to Deck 11. Everyone could read and borrow any book from the library on Deck 11. Guests could even buy some books from the shop. The collections were modern and new for anyone to read and work from.

I walked through each section of categories one by one but didn't find Joe anywhere. There was a guarded, hidden passage behind the shelves that led to the library on Deck 10.

Only shadow-workers and ship crews were allowed to enter Deck 10's library. It was where the restricted, older collections were kept safe, along with the institution's manuals and documents for every project and its technicalities. Both libraries had oxygen suction mechanisms in case of fire. When sealed, they were waterproof to avoid any records getting wet in bad weather conditions, or worse, in the event of being sunk.

There he was, classical Joe, escaping reality into a classic book. I loved watching his frowning face when he read. One time he read one, but other times he could read multiple at once. It was needed for his role to cross check references for the safety of our operations. I sat beside him on a lean back sofa in one reading space.

He pulled me by the waist to be closer to him. After he leaned me against his chest, he held his book above my belly. "What's the matter, little fish? Hmm? Still having cramps?"

"Not so much anymore. It should be the last day of my period." I gave him a kiss on the cheek.

He whispered in my ear, saying, "I'll fuck this cunt real hard until I get you pregnant, so you won't have to deal with those bloody cramps."

"Oh, Joe... But we can't right now. We're on call. You should find Sandy and tell him..." I paused to look around us, making sure that no one near us could hear. I whispered in his ear, "They want the baby in her belly. We're the baby shower gift."

His facial expression changed in an instant. "Get your comm. We're on channel 5. Keep on swimming, little fish." He put away his book, then hugged me and kissed me like no one was around. "From where did you enter the library?"

"From Deck 11, I'll be out through Deck 10."

He checked the gun in my holster and the pocket knife in my bra. "Wait 10 minutes after I leave. Morse me on comm. Use the earpiece."

He left me with the book he read earlier, *Crime and Punishment* by Dostoyevsky, the one that was published in Russian. He taught me Cyrillic years ago. I could still read it, but I didn't understand it. I hadn't started my Russian lesson yet. I waited 10 minutes, as he told me, before walking out. I dropped the book in the returning bin on my way out.

When I was close to my suite, I looked around before entering. Through my comm, I sent the Morse code on channel 5. And then I waited for his reply.

I carried my gun, my knife, and my comm. In my bum bag, I put packs of batteries and some first aid while on the move. I packed a tube of lubricant, even though it sounded illogical at a time like this. Just in case I found Lance, there was a chance he would become hungry enough to claim his cake.

I received a reply from Joe, but still nothing from Sandy. Lance was already on call status, so I wouldn't try to wait for him. The reserved crew got the status first, even before us.

18

Sealed

I got my lunch at the restaurant on Deck 7, at the back of the restaurant, near the kitchen. Finally, I received a reply from Sandy through the comm.

After I finished eating, I pretended to ask for some chocolate for my period mood. Luckily, the station chef let me into the kitchen, where I lost my trail and hid for a while. What a nice woman she was, giving me some light bites to carry. It was indeed practical since I was constantly moving around.

My period simply stopped in the afternoon, maybe because this lockdown was getting more intense than before. Since I hadn't received any updates about the fishing day we had this morning, I became more anxious by the hour.

Out of nowhere, a shadow-worker pulled me out of my way. The moment she pulled me aside, the aisle lighting was reduced. Something wasn't right because it was only around sunset.

We were heading closer to the belly of Slava, to the bulletproof aisle. We walked towards the entrance of the belly. Five shadow-workers were on guard in front of the entrance. For other parts of the ship, we had security guards, but we had shadow-workers guarding the way to the belly.

After passing the layer one entrance, we kept going through the maze until we reached the layer two entrance. Another five shadow-workers were guarding a few metres in front of the lift. We went further down to her belly, using the lift.

When it opened, five other shadow-workers welcomed us with their guns pointed at us. There were two sections inside her belly. The nuclear fusion chamber that produced our hybrid power was towards the aft, and the bunker was forward.

We walked towards the bunker entrance, where three shadow-workers were guarding it. Entering the bunker, I saw Lance in the common room. I wasn't surprised to find him here in the bunker. He was the first to be called if something happened with the active deck crew. He would be the contingency navigator in the belly if the primary bridge fell.

Once I was secured inside the bunker, she left the two of us alone. Immediately, I hugged Lance so tightly. "Lance, I miss you, you know." I *did* miss him, indeed.

"Are you all right, little star?" He showered me with kisses, giving me his warmest smile, although I knew that both of us were anxious about this uncertainty. "We're going to be all right. You hear me?"

"Lance, I need to know something. About your past, about you and Amma."

He sighed, closing his green eyes. "I know it'll catch us eventually. I don't want to hide anything from you."

"Lance..."

"Yes, little star?"

"I, um..." While cupping his face, I said, "I love you, too, Lance."

"Your schedule got delayed or what? I know that already. You don't need to be pressured to say it." He kissed me gently. "You're the most important thing in my life. Well, up until you give birth to my baby, then you'll have a competitor. At least one competitor."

I chuckled at his words, loving his humour. He knew how to tickle my nervousness. "I like competitions."

"How is your belly? Still having cramps?"

"My period just stopped. Anxious, probably. I don't know."

"Come here, you. Just stay here, being a cute, shiny little star. Leave the anxiety to me."

About half an hour later, Sandy came into the bunker carrying his duffel bag. I didn't have the chance to pack my things to be brought in all of a sudden. A few minutes later, Joe came in with two shadow-workers; one was the one who brought him in and the other was the one who brought me in.

She carried a duffel bag with my belongings inside. "These are your belongings. I packed what I thought you might need, though I'm not sure you need any clothes with these three."

Sandy rose from his seat, saying, "What did you say?" At the same time, Joe turned his face towards her, in shock that he had dropped his duffel bag.

"Oh, let's pretend that you haven't realised how good we are at doing our job to know what we need to know," said the shadow-worker who brought him in.

"No camera in the bathroom or bedroom. Not our place to judge any of your bedtime stories. Just do your job right, then we're cool with you four," she said.

Before getting weirder, I asked, "Anyone care to brief us with any updates?"

"Infiltrations. We're still on lockdown. I believe the active captain has briefed you about what they're after," she said.

"He has. About us being the target, but not about the infiltrations. Is it from the fishing day?"

"No, they're among the guests. They've been watching us from Adelaide."

"And what about the other guests?"

"Consider them our hostages, assuming they wouldn't attack the non-institutional ones. All the shadow-workers on board are spread out among the crew and offices. Also, we can't let the hostages escape, of course," she said in the most malefic way. "We'll leave the four of you sealed."

Here we were, the four of us, sealed in the bunker. "Well, I know some of them know about us. But, really? Does *everyone* need to know *everything* about our lives? I wanted to punch them in the face."

"Babe, are you sure you're off your period? I think the mood's still on," said Sandy. Immediately, he got hit in the back of his head by Joe.

"Do you need Amma's flip flop, though? She hit me a lot with that when I didn't do my homework. I mean, that thing could be lethal."

After pulling my gun from its holster, I pointed it straight at Lance. "This one could be lethal as well."

"Well, that was fast. From '*I love you, too, Lance*' to pointing a gun at me in the same hour."

"Damn, that was fast. It took us years to hear the L-word coming out."

"For the record, I was waiting for you two to come in." While giving the Ceolmund brothers their credit, I kept facing Lance since I didn't know where he stood yet. "Was it true what the captain said about you? The ship you were raised on was a spy ship, was it?"

"Of course it was. How do you think Amma and I were joining Slava? Appa Zhou made quite a name for himself. Even after he died, his reputation lives."

"Right... and serving more than one boss might be confusing in choosing a side, *innit*?"

"Surprisingly, no confusion so far."

"And which side are you on right now, if I may?"

"Always on our own side. Learnt that survival mode early on. So, please, save yourself some time. I gave it to you already."

"And what precisely did you already give me?"

He moved closer towards me and held my gun, pressing it to his chest. "Point it *here*, straight in. The heart's yours already. You might need to pull the trigger right now. Otherwise, I'm gonna make you pay later on for whatever *this* is."

He smiled when he saw me blinking. My brain was waking up from a suspicious mind. He said nothing, only smiling. A surrendering smile this time.

"Trust me, I'm with you. But I need to know if you're with me. And not with them. Whoever *them* were."

"It'll save some bullets if you simply ask about my childhood."

"Who are you, really, Lance? If you're with them, no worry, the blame's on me. I let my guard down."

"I was—uh, left in a bucket... not in a cot, but in a bucket one morning. This was what Appa told me. I think my mother, I mean, my real mother, I think she was hoping for a better life for me. We've seen everything from ugly to hell on earth. Appa and his crew weren't always selling things. That's why he gave me and Amma away to the Great One. Before he sailed for the last time, he asked for nothing in return. He loved her, you know. I was mad at him for leaving Amma. I wouldn't do that; I couldn't leave you the way he did."

"Who else knows about this?"

"Milady was the one who accepted me. You know the story with her babies. I'm sorry I didn't tell you this earlier. I couldn't stay away from you any longer. That's why I asked for a transfer."

He might not say everything, but I heard him. And I listened to everything he said to me, with or without words in between us. I paid attention to the details of his facial expression. Each small detail told the story of Lance.

"I meant it when I said, 'I love you, too,' Lance. Not simply because I needed you to talk." Realising how wrong I was for questioning his loyalty, I let go of my gun. I trusted that he wouldn't sell us that way.

"Ugh, I need a shower." Stomping on my feet, I left them in the common room. In the bathroom, I screamed my lungs out. I was glad that this bunker was soundproof. My men needed to get used to me getting weird when I had a lot on my plate. Surely, they could always serve their 'meats' at any time.

19

Well-Used

My period had ended, but I was still easily irritated. I needed a shower to wash out this intense thought in my head. With all my men being here with me in such an intense time like this, I was highly grateful.

Surely, I was excited that the four of us were in a bulletproof, soundproof bunker that could only be opened from the inside once it was sealed. No one could hear how good they would fuck me.

My men needed to have me tonight. *I* needed them to have me tonight. With the syringe, I filled myself with water. Not as much as when Sandy filled me, but enough to clean me out. Besides, I hadn't had tea, either. I took a shower after draining the water inside me to prepare myself for my men. Not quite sure why, but I liked doing it for them.

Only in a towel, I got out of the bathroom. When heading back to my men, I made sure that they saw me in it. Once I was in the bedroom, I took off the towel. On one of the beds, I opened my legs widely to show them how needy I was. "In case you didn't believe that I'm off my period, you can check it yourself."

"We're so lucky to be in this soundproof bunker. Crawl to me and take off my belt."

On all fours, I crawled towards Joe. I did as he said and then sat on my knees in front of him. I raised his belt with both of my hands, just like I was giving him an offering.

"Look at this beautiful whore, begging to be punished." He took his belt from my hands to use it on me. "You weren't nice to Lance earlier. Now turn around. Put our arse up in the air."

His belt landed on my arse. "One... Two... "

Lance lowered himself in front of me, pulling my hair back. "Whose arse is it?"

"Yours. Three... Four..." I became a meal as soon as Joe finished my first round. My hips were pulled down to feed his mouth. With Joe lying on the floor eating my pussy, his brother took out his cock to feed my mouth. Sandy pushed me back to sit on Joe's face entirely.

Sandy's length thrust into the back of my throat. "You look so beautiful when you cry like this," he said when I was gagging. "Breathe with your nose. We need you breathing."

Joe slurped every drop of my first release. "Hmm... our whore tastes so good. Leaking with so much need."

Sandy pulled his cock out of my mouth. "It's my round now." He took off his belt and was about to use it on my arse.

"Start the count." Lance was down on one knee in front of me again. This time, he held my throat. Once Sandy finished his round, Lance slapped me across the face with his other hand. Lance fucked my sobbing face while Sandy was stretching my pussy with his entire hand.

"Let me stretch our cunt here. You'll get more than one at once tonight. We need another one from our whore." He was fisting me until I squirted my second release. He smeared all my wetness on his hand along my slit and into my arse hole.

"Now, crawl towards Joe and sit on his lap. I want our cunt clenching his cock while I use my belt on you."

Joe's naked body was lying underneath me. He was to watch me have my punishment up close. "Ugh, we've never done this before. Glad to have Lance on board. He's rougher than me and Sandy."

I slid Joe inside of me before receiving my punishment for questioning my owner's loyalty. "One... Two..."

"I say this one deserves two rounds from me. You dared to question me earlier."

"Three... Please, I'm sorry. I didn't—Arrghh, Four..."

He started another round right away. "Time for me to take this arse tonight. You want this arse taken? Hmm?"

"Three... Yes, please, Lance, it's yours. Four."

With the wetness that ran down on my thigh, he prepared my arse. "You're so wet. We don't even need lubricants." He stroked my pussy alongside Joe a few times. Then he pulled his cock out and thrust it into my arse. "Fuck, so tight. Oh, this arse feels so good."

"I'm... so full." I was being pumped from the front and behind.

"Not full yet. I'm not in yet."

"Sandy, please, I'm full already. I'm—Aarrgghh. It hurts."

"Do you want us to stop? Hmm? Tell us to stop," Joe said. He knew precisely how to turn my cry into a beg for more. "Otherwise, you need to beg us to fuck you harder."

"Use your words, Mia. Say what you want us to do to our whore," Sandy said while pulling my hair with his fist.

"Oh, it hurts... Mmmh... So good. Fuck me. Harder. Please. Use me properly."

All three of them were filling and pumping me in different ways. Joe and Sandy were in my pussy and Lance was in my arse at the same time. I felt all three of them inside of me. I couldn't recall how many times I screamed at this point or how loud my screams were.

"Tell them what you are to me," Lance commanded.

"Imma—I'm Lance's sex slave."

"Oh, fuck! That means if he shares you with us or anybody else, you obey him." Sandy slipped his hand around to reach my clit.

Joe squeezed my arse to widen my holes. He said, "That means you're just a property to use anytime he wants, however he wants. He can use whatever he wants, including us, to fuck you for him."

Each of my men was vigorous in using me, which brought me so close to my second release. "Then come for us while all of us are inside you. Let us feel how hard my slave can come." Only by his words was I crying out my orgasm loudly.

Lance's hand moved from grabbing my hair to choking my neck. "Go on, get yourself off again. Hand to our clit. Give us another one," Lance said.

"I can't anymore, please."

Lance took my hand and slipped it in between me and Joe. His fingers entered my mouth.

Joe said, "The owner said one more. Slave obeys."

Once I got off another one, my owner said, "What a fucking good slave I got here. Glad these brothers shared this whore with me. Fuck, I'm close."

Lance got off first, followed by Joe, and finally Sandy. I was filled to the brim with their cum. I was so glad that they made me their whore. I was being used so well. They made me feel useful in this way.

20

Alternate Bridge

"Ugh, I must be feeling weird sitting on my bum tomorrow."

"I told you that I'd take *this* at some point." Lance keeps rubbing my arse and giving gentle massages. "What is it? Your head's elsewhere."

I raised my head while still lying on my stomach. There was something odd; I could feel it. One by one, I turned my face towards my men. Crawling towards the edge of the bed, I saw my men raise their bodies. I felt their cum leak out of me. Facing forward, I sat on the edge. My breathing was calm, but my mind wasn't. "Sandy, is it me? Or... Hmm, I think she's fast."

He sat beside me, keeping his calmness and breathing. He held my hand on his lap. We learnt this technique from my father a long time ago. To feel her movement and progress in our gut and with our bums. He used to cover our eyes with patches and our heads with flour sacks.

When he opened his eyes, Sandy looked at me and said, "She's off her course." He put on his underpants in a hurry.

"Joe, pull out the camera view of the bridge. Lance, find out where she's going." I put my knickers on, and I grabbed the shirt that was closest to me, regardless of who it belonged to.

All of us rushed towards the alternate bridge. None of us were wearing footwear. Once Joe pulled out the view on the screen, none of the cameras were showing anything. Clearly, something was off at this point.

"Joe, do we still have the hidden camera? Pull them out slowly, one by one."

Only the first to fourth in command knew where the hidden cameras were. Some of them were already in place; others were retractable and concealed.

The four of us cursed almost at the same time when we saw the hidden camera feed. The primary bridge had fallen. It was a bloodbath for the active crew. They were all murdered.

There were three men controlling the primary bridge, but we didn't know who they were yet. Then the voice came out of the speakers. All video and audio were one way. We could see and hear them, but they couldn't have anything from us. As they put our communication out loud, we couldn't send any messages to anyone on the channel.

"Joe, pull out the external cameras. Let me see what she sees."

The lighting inside the alternate bridge was reduced to allow us to see the environment better. It was already night outside. There was a reason why the alternate bridge made me feel like I was inside an igloo. This bridge had a dome ceiling and wall to display views from the projector above our heads. It looked like a vintage disco ball, if you ask me.

"Fuck, we're in the open ocean," Lance said.

"Keep me updated if anyone tries to enter the belly," I said to Joe.

"On it." He paused, frowning at his display. "Weird. I don't think anyone's aware that the bridge has fallen. I'll keep listening."

"Sandy, sync us with primary. Anyone, don't change or move anything." We paused any movement, waiting for both decks to sync. All readings, displays, and settings in the alternate were the same as the ones in the primary.

"Bearing 265. Where the fuck are they pushing her? Seriously, these arseholes thought they could reach Cape Town without anyone noticing, or what?"

I turned my face from Lance towards Joe. "Any break in?"

"Negative. What's your plan?"

"It was their suicide mission, then. They would need refuelling with this state of fuel unless they were planning on hybrids. Are they sealed inside the bridge?"

Joe replied, "No, it's open. Do you want to seal them inside?"

"Yes, seal them. Lance, set a secondary course for Freemantle. Be ready. Once we take over control, activate the secondary."

"Gas is ready. Do you want to dismantle or take them out entirely?"

"Dismantle only. The institution might need information on why they wanted to sink us."

"Sandy, play classics on the speaker, ship wide. Play anything Bach first, the short ones, then Requiem." Bach would tell the shadow-workers that there had been chaos and that the communication channel was no longer secure. They would use sign language from this moment on.

By the time Mozart was played, more shadow-workers started guarding the belly. Requiem would tell them that the primary bridge had fallen. Five of them guarded each layer of entrance; another five guarded our fusion chamber;

and five guarded us outside the alternate bridge. Shadow-workers started to go towards the primary bridge. They didn't know about our plan yet.

"They can't get in, Joe. They're not wearing any gas masks." I watched the feed from the outside of the deck. "Lights. Sandy, Morse them. Joe, standby for gas."

We sort of held our breath at this point.

"They got the codes," Sandy said.

"Lance, standby on nav. Joe, gas in three, two, one." We waited for those three pirates to pass out before taking over control.

"Set heading 055," I said, commanding Lance.

"Heading 055, Set."

"Reduce speed for the turn. All clear?"

"Clear to turn."

"Port heading 055." She was turning so calmly that I kept watching my display and the dome projection in turns.

"Time," said Lance while starting the count when she reached her intended heading.

"Set next heading 085."

Sandy looked at me to warn me. "Wind. Northerly, at 16-20 knots."

"Advise heading 080. Ten seconds to go," Lance said.

I commanded, "Set heading 075."

Lance called out, "Heading 075, Set. Clear to turn. Five seconds to go."

"Turn to heading 075."

"Heading 075."

I watched the display on Lance's side. "Increase speed. We're too far out of Freemantle."

"Speed increased."

"Get her on track. When she's on track, turn to heading 080." I turned my face towards Joe and said, "Clear the gas from the primary bridge. Once it's clear, open the seal."

We watched the shadow-workers enter the primary deck. They checked if there was any surviving crew. So I picked up the phone to call the primary deck. One of the shadow-workers picked up the phone but kept himself silent.

"Bridge, this is Captain Phinnisee. We've got eyes. Anyone active who survives?"

He shook his head to answer my question.

"I have control. Request frequency."

He signed for the secure radio frequency.

"Request frequency."

He signed it one more time to make sure that we had the correct one. He signed us to sail towards Freemantle but to wait for further information before porting.

"I have control of the mothership. You have all her decks. We're all ears."

We watched them bring out the three pirates from the primary bridge. Once they were out of the primary bridge, we sealed it closed. We retracted the hidden cameras and turned off the feed.

"Heading 080, Set."

"Stand by, Lance. Sandy, fuel on board?"

"They've burned way more than she needed. She still has her reserve. Do we go on the bat?"

"Keep the reserved fuel. We go electric."

"Bats are standing by."

"Prepare the chamber before we switch on the bat."

Once we switched on the bat, we saw the entire ship going dark except for us in the belly. About three seconds later, Slava lit herself up once again.

"Engine, stabilised. Chamber's ready to recharge."

"Lance, turn to heading 080. Sandy, maintain her speed. Joe, keep your eyes and ears on the shadow-workers. Ugh, I need to go pee. I'm not even wearing any trousers."

That was their first smile after an intense event. How I loved them—my crew, my men.

"Then go pee, little fish. We've got your bridge here, Captain."

"Sandy, you have control."

"My mothership," Sandy responded when I handed over the control.

21

The Surprising Visit

Going out of the bathroom, I was fully clothed with my handgun in the holster, just in case the thing got worse. I returned to the alternate bridge, only to find all three of them getting intense. Indeed, things were getting worse.

"Anyone who wants to use the loo should get the shoes and guns on the way back here. I'll watch."

"No, I'll stay. Hey Sandy, get my shoes and gun, will you?"

"Got it."

"I'll get something for us to eat. We haven't got any."

Joe and I kept watching the feed of two people with long, black, hooded cloaks. They had their swords sheathed behind their spines. They wore sturdy, bulletproof black armour underneath their cloaks. Some shadow-workers shot them, but the bullets just fell off. They dismantled the shadow-workers who were on their way to the belly of Slava.

Sandy and Lance returned to the alternate bridge and locked the door behind us. Joe kept watching the feed while wearing his shirt and having his gun on his waist.

They went through the first and second layers of the belly. From how they walked and dismantled those shadow-workers, they were a man and a woman. We couldn't see their faces since they were wearing black face masks.

"Holy shit! Who are these guys? Are we still sealed, Joe?"

They just exited the lift and passed through the third layer. We watched to see if they turned to the nuclear fusion chamber or the contingency deck. They turned forward—to us.

"Yes, we are. Lance, guard with me. Sandy, you're still the second in command."

All the guards were down. And just like that, the man opened the door to the bunker, as if he knew the key to it. Supposedly, the bunker could only be opened from the inside once it was sealed.

Joe and Lance walked closer to the door. All of us pulled out our guns and pointed them towards the door. That man closed the door and locked it once they were inside the bunker. And again, he opened the door to the alternate bridge from the outside.

Once inside, he pulled the guns from Joe and Lance. He choked on their necks with his bare hands. The woman pulled Sandy's gun within seconds. She pointed the gun at him while choking on my neck. Sandy raised his hands, surrendering, terrified that she would hurt me.

She lifted me by the neck, which made me tip toe. "Drop the gun into your holster, little missy."

I saw her green eyes turning red. Dropping my gun, I reached for her hand, catching some air to breathe. "Milady."

"This.is.not.a brothel house. It smells like sex here. From what I heard, every man in this room has been sharing your cunt," Milady said.

"My.love. I did no such thing," said the Great One.

Milady chuckled at her husband's words. Her red eyes returned to green once again. "My lovely Angel, you are not a man. And please, I'm trying to give them some terror here."

"Apologise. My bad. Please proceed, my love."

She released my neck and gave the gun back to Sandy. "You sort of ruined the mood already," Milady said with a spoiled whining voice to her husband.

She took off her face mask and hood, showing off her beautiful features. She was the kind of woman I looked up to. She knew how to be a girl boss but was so feminine around her husband. Milady knew how to balance between the two. Although those people made Lilith one of the symbols of feminism, I saw her differently in person. She wasn't like the later wave of feminists who leaned more towards becoming almost all-against-men.

She was a woman of power, but she became a loving and nurturing wife to our Great One. She was intelligent but always listened to her husband with full attention and curiosity. And the way she sounded and moved around her husband, she might be misunderstood by others as a naive young woman with her sugar Daddy.

While trying to catch my breath, I said, "Milady, my Great One, what a surprising visit tonight. How can we assist you?"

The Great One released Joe and Lance from the grip of his hands. "Firstly, by not gassing our reserved crews for them to pass out. That would have been helpful. Thankfully, you didn't gas them longer. Otherwise, we would need another round of recruitment."

"Wait, what? I thought they were pirates. If only I—"

"If only you weren't so occupied spreading your legs, little missy, you could have played back the recording," said Milady.

"Precisely the reason why Lilith and I always have more than one set of reserved crews on board. Well, just in case you're too occupied. Besides, we've learnt from history to have contingency plans. Plural."

"If they're your reserved crew, then who was the pirate?" I was bombarded with straight, sarcastic faces that the Great One and Milady gave me. "Wait, what? The active crew? The captain?"

"Huh... It seems so surprising to you that a captain can have so much power. These younglings are so naive sometimes." The Great One massaged his forehead just like he couldn't believe how foolish we were.

Milady stepped closer to me. "If you switch sides, these three would follow your cunt. Be careful who you spread your legs for. Cunts can be dangerous for fucking men's brains."

"But that didn't make any sense. The captain warned me about us being the targets. And he told me that someone put a 15 million pounds price tag on Slava. And then I told my crew."

"Did he warn you, or was he trying to turn you around? You've got to be able to tell the difference, little missy."

As much as I didn't like being called that way, like a fool, she deserved to call me that. Maybe I was a fool for being so naive. I continued, "And he had all the crew following him, really?"

I clearly saw their grins; even without any words, I got what they meant. Then I turned my face towards my crew one by one, saying, "Don't you dare switch sides, any of you! Otherwise, I'll rip your balls off and shove them into each other's throats. Not your own balls... each other's balls."

My men were shaking their heads and putting their hands in the air, surrendering. I tried hard to contain my laughter. They were helplessly in love with me, and I was so grateful for each one of them. That was because I was in love with each of them as well.

When I turned my face away from my men, Milady caught me by surprise. She was kissing and lapping my lips vigorously. "That's my good girl."

The Great One dropped his jaw while watching us. "Fuck, that.is.hot!" My men, at the same time, nodded and licked their lips.

"First things first, let me know if you're expecting any babies."

"Milady?"

"I can smell their cum on you. Clearly, they weren't wearing anything. Well, I can't be visiting here while you are having newborns. It can be dangerous for their health. Once they're a month older, they'll be all right. You can bring them on board while you're working. Don't give any of these men any free pass for not doing their roles in raising their offspring."

"Milady, you don't feel weird about us four?"

She turned her face towards her husband. "We've been living long enough not to judge something and brand it as weird."

"Besides, in the Far North, there was a wife-swapping tradition. Their family sort of raised their children together. Let's say that there were more hands to help one another. Practical for their survival over there," the Great One said.

Joe responded, "I've read some about *nevtumgyt* in the library. They're quite fascinating about building a solid family together as a unit but separating the genes from one another. Not quite sure how the blood pact worked, though."

"Ah, gladly, this youngling can read. Well, the indigenous also practise adopting their brothers' children after their passing, if that concerns you."

"The orphan has no objection to either of you adopting my children when I'm gone," Lance said.

"Can anyone include me in the baby talk at the least?"

"Ah, yes, Captain. Of course, you'll still be their mother. Your voice should matter. In the meantime, no altogether action when you're an active crew set. Someone needs to be on the bridge."

"Understood, My Great One, Milady. If I may ask... I thought the bunker could only be opened from the inside once it was sealed. How—"

"I built this ship, didn't I? Lilith and I are the only two beings who can open it from the outside."

I nodded my understanding to him. "And where do we go from here?"

"Resume normal operations. Australia was a decoy, to get more operative shadow-workers on the ground and leave Slava mostly with the injured ones."

"Understood, my Great One."

"Fuck, these new armours are tight."

"We should tell the maker to get yours adjusted, my love."

"Surely it wasn't tight until you kissed her, little bird. Look what you've done to me," he said while pulling his wife close to his raging bulge.

"That one, I can help you with."

He carried her on his shoulder. It seemed primal but pure, with desire and love. Although the bunker was soundproof for anyone on the outside to hear anything, all four of us inside here could surely hear them fuck.

They were different beings than us, so I believed none of us would stand the intensity of their fuck. The way the Great One dominated his wife was nothing like I'd ever heard before. An hour of them fucking felt like forever to the four of us listening.

The way she whimpered, moaned, and screamed sounded like the translation of everything I had inside my heart and my head. It was the same tiredness that I had from being the primary decision maker on my duty.

Her begs were translations of my weariness as a woman of power. It was the same way I begged my men to take over the power to control my body. There was this tiredness and exhaustion of the control I got from duty that I needed to let go of and pass on to my men to hold. Not everyone understood what it took to stay strong all the time as a woman on top of the career ladder. I begged my men to let me submit myself to them.

We then continued our schedule to port in Freemantle. From there, we continued the fishing day to get more injured shadow-workers and treat them on board. We made more stops to catch as many as we could.

The Great One and his wife stayed on board. After half of the injured were recovered, we were given briefings and retraining about the event and how to prevent it from happening again in the future. Scenarios were built and mitigated for us to learn from. Joe was pulled into those retraining sessions since he handled safety in operations.

Milady seemed to enjoy her time on board. And she cooked a lot for us—three meals and two light meals. She was ancient and knew traditional recipes as they were originally made. Surely, Amma enjoyed her learning time with Milady; I could see it on her face.

Epilogue

Thankfully, we arrived in Lombok even earlier than our original schedule. All was the courtesy of Lance. I wouldn't trade him for any other navigator, especially not after he joined our bed. I would keep him.

"Go see, Mandy. We got this, baby girl."

"Your mothership, Sandy."

"Aye." He nodded, giving me a reassuring smile.

"If the governor's princess is the one you're so excited to see, you need to take it outside, Captain." Our Great One pulled his bright sky eyes away from the binoculars. He looked at me with his arms crossed.

Only one of my feet almost stepped outside the primary bridge, so I stopped myself. While moving backwards, I asked him, "Is there anything about her that we should be concerned about? She and I are practically sisters. Not by birth, at least, but close to it. She sounded different on our last phone call. Different bad."

"She isn't my concern. Yours, nonetheless." He turned his body towards Mandy at the port.

"Then I shall see her *outside*, as you wish."

Our Great One continued, "Captain, Older Ceolmund, it's her watchdog that might be concerning for our operation. As far as the princess's safety goes, she's in good hands. But that lone wolf she has can be lethal."

Joe turned his head towards me. I could feel him locking his eyes on me. "Understood, our Great One. I'll help Captain Phinnisee take the measurements."

There were no words coming out of my lips. I didn't know how to respond to that kind of information. I didn't even know what to think.

Mandy had already returned here for almost a year. Even with so many employees in her company, or even with a bodyguard following her everywhere, I could tell that she had been alone. She surely had lost some sleep by the way her panda eyes looked; the dark circles gave some puffiness around her grey eyes. She was restless, escaping from earth into her towering, high paperwork. It was the only escapism she understood. It only became seamless because they were now digital.

"Oh, I've missed you so much, cupcake."

She chuckled. "Please don't tell me you've asked someone to make me some cupcakes."

"Indeed, I have." I took out a cupcake from the box. "No worry, dear. I brought four here, in case you want to get your watchman fat."

She talked with her mouth full of cake. "Owh, Max, this is Mia. Mmhh, it tastes good. I sowwwyy, couldn't help it."

"Saint. Max Saint. Nah, I'm good with the cake. She can have all of them. So where to?"

"Oh, we can't board the ship. They're a bit occupied cleaning up from Australia."

"So I've heard Australia was a bit of a handful. I hope it wasn't out of hands, Captain."

I had no clue what he heard or from whom he heard it. I wondered if this was what the Great One said about him. "Well, each journey has its own challenges. But I'd follow Mandy on this one. We're lucky enough she shoves those cupcakes in her mouth."

"Glad we're on the same boat." He looked at her through the mirror. "Where to, princess?"

"Is there something between them?"

While chewing, she said, "Umh, I trust you, Max."

Immediately, I turned my face towards Mandy. She was always having a hard time trusting people. Either my ears were ringing, so I thought I heard her saying that she trusted him, or there was *definitely* something between them.

She asked me rhetorically, "What?"

"Nothing. Nice to know you've learnt how to trust anyone on planet Earth."

Mandy, indeed, had a birthright to the title, but the way he called her princess was different. It was like he called her *his* princess. And the way her body moved was different around him. She let go of her control so that he could almost Daddy her.

As she said on the phone, he was older than her. I agreed that Max looked like he was 33 years old. But I had met ex-military shadow-workers, so I knew that there was something that he buried underneath those calms before the storm. Either he was actually older or he was on a specific MOS that required him to be unreadable.

Max stopped at a restaurant near the beach. He must had learnt that they served the freshest seafood here. "Is this one okay? People in the office wouldn't know how to handle her sugar rush tomorrow. At least with seafood, she can be as salty as she wishes."

"Of course. She can crack those crabs open. Or cracking open whatever it is she has in her head." I turned to look at her. "Well, you can't be crabby all the time, you see."

"Again, we're on the same boat," Max agreed, implying that we shared the same concerns.

She looked at us in turns before he opened his door. "What is it with you two implying everything in every sentence you speak?"

"Some aspects of seamanship have similar occupational hazards as the armed forces. So we learnt to deliver messages without being caught."

"So, I've heard."

After opening the door for her, he said, "Oh, you got some icing on there. Let me... I got you."

Although I was glad that someone cared for her, nobody paid a bodyguard to care about cake frosting, just like what I saw. The waitress found two tables for us quickly. Mandy and I sat a few tables away from Max. He was sitting towards the front entrance to continue looking out.

Mandy talked a lot about her father's matchmaking plan. So I asked her about how much Max knew about it and if what she said was true about trusting him. At some point in our messy supper, Mandy was struggling to crack the crab open. I locked my eyes on Max's eyes intentionally. Then I looked at my left hand and returned to look at him in the eyes. I could only hope that he would understand.

When Mandy finally cracked open the crab, she continued telling me her story. Somehow, I became more concerned about her now than before meeting her. I went to the loo when I felt full—full from eating and full of thoughts about her.

When I got out of the loo, Max was already there, in the shadow, looking outside, doing his job. "I almost thought you didn't get the message."

"Morse code was one of the basics."

"Did you sign any non-disclosure agreements when you got hired?"

"Yes." He didn't respond further, only anticipating what was needed to be said or asked.

"There's no trust law in this country. Her father was concerned that whoever married her would get his hands on her money. And let's not forget everything her father has once he dies. So he put everything under the holding company. It was done right after her parents' messy divorce."

"I'm listening."

"Also, this country acknowledges that husbands will be the patrons of their wives. Fathers have less power once their daughters are married. So I assume that it was the holding company that hired you on the paper."

"I can neither confirm nor deny your assumption. You've heard me, NDA."

"That's my point. To protect the CEO, *her*, from whoever is potentially harming her. It doesn't matter if it was her future husband *or* her own father."

"Is the princess herself a threat?"

"Your judgement, Saint; if that is even your real name. If it isn't, you better live up to the name."

"Saints patronise and protect."

"Huh, glad to know the 'serve and protect' never left this soldier."

"And you're suggesting what?"

I sighed, delaying my next sentence. "She wasn't built the way we were, Saint. She doesn't even have contingency plans. So she doesn't scatter a little bit of something across the world. *If she decides to leave, she'll bring nothing but whatever she wears that day.*"

Background Stories

The story of this book, "A Sailing Legacy: Adventures of the Sea Captain," was inspired by the folktale "Two Brothers and the Sailor." In the original folktale, the sailor only picked up one brother and left the other one. Because of that, the author and the publisher felt that the story of the one who was left behind wasn't finished yet.

We might find some similarities in this tale with the one in the Portuguese folktale, considering some historical events in the past. The characters in this book themselves were built from different types of traditional ships and boats.

The names Zhou and Ceolmund meant ship or boat, while Mia's last name was derived from a type of ship called *Pinisi*. It was a modification of a traditional Celebes ship. Portuguese ships had an influence on this type of ship. People from the South Celebes started to make the early version of the ship for fishing. With modifications, people started to use the ship for cargo or even as a merchant ship. There were rituals for building the ship.

The ability of the ship to change its functions and purposes in response to circumstances served as inspiration for and helped create the character Mia Phinnisee. The ship continued to set sail to this day.

The traditional South Borneo fishing boat known as *Jukung* served as an inspiration for Joe-Kung Ceolmund. The ship had been around since the tenth century AD. The earlier spelling used /oe/ for the letter u. This type of small boat was to provide the community with fishing in rivers and lakes. This ship inspired the author to build the character of Joe in the story, who had the traits of a provider.

The *Sandeq* boat from West Celebes, which has been around since the nineteenth century AD, served as the inspiration for the character Sandec Ceolmund. This type of fishing boat was one of the fastest traditional boats in the world. The boat was designed sleekly to reach faster as Sandy accelerated in his training and climbed the ranks higher than his brother Joe.

Both Jukung and Sandeq boats were stabilised by having two outriggers. That became the foundation of how the two brothers in the books built a stable home for Mia.

Pantchiallang, a massive merchant ship, served as the foundation and inspiration for Lance's character. People in the Riau archipelago built this type of ship. Another version of this type of ship was called the *Lancang Kuning*, which had dragons as decorations at the front and stern. The ship could also be read in the tale of Hang Tuah.

Lancang Kuning was for the Sultan to travel or go for a battle. *Kuning* meant yellow, so it was only right for Lance to have blond hair. His green eyes represented the prosperity of merchants.

Being tall and sharp in times of war, *Pantchiallang* served its purpose of spying on the enemy by being a merchant ship on the outside. That multipurpose ship built the foundation for the complex operation of Slava. The name Slava meant "Glory," because *Lancang Kuning* was indeed built for glory.

About the Author

Rada Lyubomirova retells the myths, legends, and folktales with a darker taste and morally grey characters. Each story is to reimagine childhood stories in either historical or contemporary literary art. Her works are to give rebirth to the timeless narratives that have enthralled generations.

Her writing style is a tasteful blend of dark romance with a medium-to-fast burn rate. Classic stories are given a seductively darker twist to guide you with a passion that will keep you delightfully hooked deep into the night.

As the author enjoys her travel time, her books invite you to take an enchanting journey through exotic lands to return to treasured childhood memories. By meeting people from different cultural backgrounds, the author finds that myths, legends, and folktales may unite people.

Through exploring foreign lands, the author sees the commonalities that connect cultures through stories. She finds it fascinating how these tales travel across borders and unite people in a sense of wonder and value to pass down to the next generation.

Rada cherishes the bond and collaboration she has with her readers. Your feedback shapes and enhances the realms she creates in the literary arts. Is there another tale, legend, or folktale that has fascinated you? Leave your thoughts and reviews on her stories.

About the Publisher

Besides publishing fiction and non-fiction books, Compendia Publishing creates content for social media and online courses.

Scan the QR code above to see our portfolio of work.

***

Thank you for purchasing the original copy of this book.
Your feedback will help both the author and the publisher with future works.